**Then came War Day Minus Four, when
They threw in the civilians.**

Women holding babies, old people who could
barely walk, staggering along with their belongings, children fumbling onto the battlefield where
land mines blew them apart. And beautiful girls,
with haunting eyes, who held out their arms,
beseeching him. He wanted to move the civilians
to safety, but Mendor the Stern Father bellowed at
him, "Forget those people! They are not your job.
You are responsible only for your troops. Civilians
mean nothing! Do you want to lose the War?"

The Virtual War Chronologs

Virtual War [Book 1]

The Clones [Book 2]

Virtual War

THE VIRTUAL WAR CHRONOLOGS
BOOK 1

[GLORIA SKURZYNSKI]

Simon Pulse
New York London Toronto Sydney Singapore

For Edite Kroll, friend and guide

This Simon Pulse edition January 2004

First paperback edition February 1999
Copyright © 1997 by Gloria Skurzynski

SIMON PULSE
An imprint of Simon & Schuster
Children's Publishing Division
1230 Avenue of the Americas
New York, NY 10020

Also available in a Simon & Schuster Books for Young Readers hardcover edition.
Designed by Russell Gordon
The text of this book was set in Aldine 401.

Printed in the United States of America
2 4 6 8 10 9 7 5 3 1

The Library of Congress has cataloged the hardcover edition as follows:
Skurzynski, Gloria.
Virtual war / Gloria Skurzynski.
        p.   cm.
Summary: In a future world where global contamination has necessitated limited human contact, three young people with unique genetically engineered abilities are teamed up to wage war in virtual reality.
ISBN 0-689-81374-0 (hc)
[1. Science fiction. 2. Virtual reality—Fiction.] I. Title.
PZ7.S6287Vi 1997
[Fic]—dc21 96-35346
ISBN 0-689-86785-9 (pbk)
ISBN 978-1-416-97577-9

Virtual War

One

The sky was golden.

Corgan could feel sand beneath his fingers. What were those trees called, he wondered, the tall ones that curved to the sky. Ridges circled their trunks all the way up, but there were no branches or leaves except right at the top, where fingerlike green blades stuck out. . . .

What does it matter, he thought. Things don't need names. They haven't told me the names of lots of things, and I don't really care. It's nice to lie here like this under the sky and the trees and not have to practice for a while.

Someone came toward him—a girl, striding across the sand.

Her hair was more golden than the sky. As she walked, her long hair swung from side to side, swirling around her shoulders. A Go-ball racket dangled from her right hand.

She stopped right above him and looked down at him. "Want to play?" she asked.

"Sure!"

As he leaped up, he noticed with some surprise that his LiteSuit had begun to shimmer with the color of blood. Corgan knew what blood looked like. Once, a few months ago, as he'd walked along the tunnel from his Box to his Clean Room, a tile fell from the ceiling and hit his hand. His knuckles had bled, the first and only time he'd ever seen real blood.

The way the Supreme Council had carried on, it was as if Corgan's arm had been chopped off or something. About a dozen times a day They'd examined his hand to make sure it wasn't infected, even though it was only a little cut and it healed fast and felt fine. They'd moved him to a new Box at a different location—Corgan wasn't sure where. The tunnel connecting his new Box to his new Clean Room was now made of polished steel, with no tiles that could fall off, and Corgan's new Clean Room was so sterile his nose twitched every time he used it. He was just now getting used to the anti-septic smell.

"Who are you?" Corgan asked the girl as a Go-ball court materialized around them. It was a clay court—Corgan liked that. Even though Go-ball courts were created entirely from electronic impulses, virtual clay felt different underfoot than, say, virtual concrete or virtual grass.

"Sharla," she answered. "That's my name. Do you want to lead off, or should I?"

"Go ahead."

She served the ball so fast Corgan was caught off balance. He recovered and shot it back, but right from the start his timing was off. Sharla was good. Really good. They had been giving him better and better opponents over the past few months, even though Corgan's specialty wasn't Go-ball so it didn't matter too much if he didn't win. Sharla was the best opponent he'd had so far.

She ran, covering the court in wide zigzag leaps. She whacked the ball harder than anyone he'd ever practiced with.

She distracted him. Not because she did anything against the rules—Corgan felt off balance because he'd never before played against a girl his own age. Boys, men, women, robots, anything They could dream up to create an image of, no matter how unreal. But this was the first time he'd played against the virtual image of a girl who looked about—

"How old are you?" he asked.

"Fourteen," she said. "Same as you."

Wondering how she knew that, he reached out to snare a wild shot and ended up smashing the ball into the net. Since the net was shaped from thin, intersecting beams of laser light, it sparked when the ball hit it. Brilliant reds and blues and greens arced and burst like tiny flowering comets that fell to the court, where they sparked again.

"Point!" she called.

Corgan stalled. "I don't know why They bother

3

with all those flashing lights and everything when a ball hits the net," he mentioned. "It's kind of a waste of laser energy—"

"Do you hit the net often, Corgan?" she asked. "The idea is to knock the ball *over* the net." And she laughed.

The laugh sounded rich and impulsive and free; Corgan was so caught up in the sound of it that when Sharla served again, the ball flew past his ear.

He really was trying. But he couldn't keep his eyes on the ball. Sharla's pale green LiteSuit ended inches above her knees. All the females Corgan had ever played against before had been covered to the ankles with regulation LiteSuits. He wasn't used to seeing female legs, and Sharla's were . . . were . . . he didn't have a word for them. As she raced across the court, he noticed how her arms and chest twisted with every swing, how her face lighted with amusement when she hit the ball so hard it ricocheted off his forehead. If They had turned on the tactile simulator just then—if the ball had actually hit him on the head that hard—Corgan would have been knocked flat.

She laughed again, bending forward with her hands on her knees as if to keep herself from collapsing with mirth.

There was no sense pretending. He'd lost the game, dismally! "Sharla, are you real?" he shouted.

"Yes, I'm real. But They've made me look better in this image than I do in . . ."

Immediately she vanished.

Corgan felt a stab of disappointment, quickly replaced by guilt as Mendor's stern image materialized in front of him. This time Mendor was a man, the reproachful Father Figure.

"What happened?" Mendor asked. "That's the worst you've ever played."

Corgan shrugged.

"The War is less than eighteen days away."

"I know when the War is, Mendor. Seventeen days, twenty-one hours, thirty-nine minutes and forty-seven and twenty-three hundredths seconds from now."

"The War scene can contain any legal diversion, you know, including the image of a beautiful girl," Mendor continued. "Are you going to be so easily thrown off when you're fighting the real War?"

"No, I won't be," Corgan muttered. "But it was only Go-ball. . . ."

"This is serious, Corgan. You lost your concentration. That can't happen."

"Then bring her back and let me play her again," Corgan said. "I'll do better next time. It's just—I was lying on the sand, and the sun warmed me and the breeze felt good and those trees. . . . Mendor, what are those trees called?"

"Palm trees." Mendor's look softened. "It was a test, it's true. They were afraid you might be rattled by a pretty female. I told Them it wouldn't happen. 'Not Corgan,' I told Them. 'You can trust Corgan to keep his concentration, no matter what,' I told Them. 'Corgan always plays to win, no matter who his opponent is. You can count on Corgan,' I said—"

"Enough!" Corgan shouted. "Let me play Sharla again, Mendor. I'll *crush* her this time."

"Not now." Mendor's voice grew lighter and higher. As Mendor slowly morphed into a woman, into the Mother Figure, Corgan felt a trickle of approval brush him. Then Mendor morphed completely, becoming Mother Comforter, Mother Nourisher, with gentle features and tender eyes. "You're forgiven for losing," she said. "Go into your Clean Room now. You raised some sweat in that game with Sharla, and you need sanitizing. We'll see what happens after that. Maybe in an hour or so They'll let you play a game with a different girl."

"I want to play Sharla again."

Mendor's voice deepened. "Sharla is in Reprimand."

"Because of what she said? She was telling the truth, wasn't she? Don't let Them keep her in Reprimand, Mendor! Not for telling the truth!"

Mendor's maternal voice said, "I'm sure They'll consider your request, Corgan. Now go to your Clean Room."

Disgruntled, Corgan opened the door of his Box and stepped into the tunnel. He'd lost the argument with Mendor and before that he'd lost the game with Sharla. Corgan wasn't used to losing. His straight black eyebrows pulled together in a frown.

The polished steel of the tunnel reflected his scowl as he strode to his Clean Room, only a few meters away. No curves in his path, no corners, no loose tiles. A sensor opened the Clean Room door when he came close enough to it.

Clean Rooms were always built in clusters. Corgan couldn't remember where he'd picked up that bit of information; it wasn't something he'd have learned in his regular lessons. One time, four years ago, when he was only ten, he'd let himself think about it: that on the other side of the walls of his Clean Room were other Clean Rooms with other people in them, maybe sometimes using them at the same time Corgan used his. That day he'd banged on the wall while he was being sanitized, just to hear whether someone would bang back.

Never again! He'd gotten into so much trouble— Mendor the Angry Father had used his deepest, loudest voice to chastise Corgan for a full five minutes, the longest scolding Corgan had ever known in his life. Corgan had cried for hours until Mendor finally relented and morphed into the Mother Comforter, wiping his tears away.

"Haven't They given you everything a ten-year-old boy could ever want?" Mendor the

Mother Figure had asked that day. "You have toys. You have games. You have me to love you and teach you. You can create whatever playmates you want—dogs or monkeys or dolphins or other children or anything at all that your imagination can picture. All you have to do is ask and they appear in your Box, one at a time or a whole roomful of images."

All that was true. Corgan didn't know what had possessed him to bang on that wall, just to see if there'd be an answer. In the four years since then, he'd never tried it again.

Now he moved to the flush tube to pass his body fluids and solids. From there it was just one step to stand beneath the vapor nozzle. Dropping his LiteSuit to the floor, he got a quick look at his body, reflected by the stainless-steel walls. Thin. Tall. Strong legs. Shoulders needed thickening, but Mendor said Corgan couldn't expect that until a year or two more had gone by. After the War. Corgan's hands looked too big, all out of proportion to his thin arms. The fingers were long, agile, and powerful. Not much hair on his body yet, but the hair on his head stood up thick and straight and black as midnight. He flexed the muscles of his back and upper arms, pleased by the swell of his biceps. At once, the warm, cleansing vapor flowed from the nozzle above him, enveloping him. Corgan could no longer see his reflection because of steam.

He felt his head gently lifted as his hair was laser trimmed; a week had passed since the last trim. Each hair on his head had to be kept precisely five centimeters long, because that was the ideal length for cleanliness.

Hair. He thought of the girl, Sharla, and her long golden hair that swung across her shoulders as she bounded around the clay court. Was her hair really that long, or was it just the way They made her look in the virtual image? And if her hair really was that length, then why were girls allowed to wear it like that? Didn't they need to be kept clean, too? He'd have to ask Mendor.

As the vapor cleansing continued, lifting off his sweat, pulling it up into the remover pipe, Corgan pictured Sharla in his mind. The golden light had created shadows that sculpted her legs—they'd looked so lean and clean and smooth, from the calves to the thighs. . . . Was *that* part of her image real?

Suddenly the vapor that enveloped him turned icy cold.

"Hey! Stop that! I'm freezing!" Corgan yelled to his Clean Room. He was tempted to bang on the wall because the vapor cleanser had obviously malfunctioned, but he stopped himself just in time. Mendor might think Corgan was trying to communicate with someone in an adjoining Clean Room, the way he'd done four years ago. Mendor was already disgruntled because of Corgan's poor performance in the game with Sharla. Corgan didn't want to be criticized twice in one day.

His LiteSuit had dissolved and disappeared into the remover pipe. A new LiteSuit hung on a hook—shimmery blue, his favorite color. They must be trying to make amends for the icy vapor bath. Corgan frowned a little to let Them know, if They were watching, that he was still a bit unhappy with Them. After all, he was Their champion. He deserved better than a malfunctioning Clean Room and a cold vapor bath.

Back in his Box, Corgan suspended himself in the aerogel and relaxed, ready to have lunch. He turned on his favorite surround scene: ocean waves. Towering breakers rushed up to him, curled above him in crests of foam, and receded, soothing him with the throb of crashing water.

"Lunch?" he asked out loud. "Where's lunch?"

"Not yet." It was Mendor's voice, nothing more than the voice, without any face or body showing. Mendor did that sometimes. "You need reflex practice, Corgan."

Corgan sighed and turned off the ocean. Mendor was evidently in his Father Figure mode again. "Practice by myself or against a competitor?" Corgan asked.

"Competitor."

The Box crackled with laser light. "Bees," he told Mendor. "Make it bees to start out with." Corgan liked swatting at the golden bees when they darted at him, faster and faster, as they tried to sting him. They never hurt. It was just a game to check the speed of Corgan's reflexes, to challenge him at each escalating level as the program became faster and more complex. He'd never lost yet. "Bees, Mendor? Okay?"

But Mendor wasn't in an agreeable mood. "You'll practice on whatever They decide you need," he said sternly.

All right, Corgan thought. I'll show the Supreme Council. Let Them throw everything They've got at me. I'll beat Their program like I always do. I'll destruct it so bad they'll have to design it all over again.

"State your pledge," Mendor ordered.

Corgan raised his hand. "I pledge to wage the War with courage, dedication, and honor." He'd said the words so many times he no longer thought about them. "Ready!" he shouted.

"Right hand!" Mendor barked. "In place! Go!"

Lasers bombarded him, the points of light crossing his field of vision so rapidly they were almost invisible. One after another Corgan hit them with his fingertips, making them flare and die the instant he touched them.

"Left hand, middle finger!" Mendor yelled. "Faster!"

Corgan was surprised. To go straight from right hand to left hand, middle finger with no index-finger warm-up of either hand was unusual. This had been an unusual day right from the start, and it wasn't yet lunchtime. But even without a warm-up, he had no trouble making fingertip contact with the points of laser light.

"Both hands, little fingers!"

Ordinarily it wouldn't have been a difficult exercise, but suddenly they doubled the speed of the laser-light points. Corgan had to block everything else from his mind, had to focus intently on the split-second light attack. They tried to trick him by adding colors—They weren't supposed to do that. According to the rules, no more than four colors could appear on the field at a single time. Still, he never missed a point.

A terrible laugh made his arm hairs stand up. A monstrous face appeared in front of him. Steady, he told himself, it's just an illusion; They're trying to break my concentration. The maniacal laughter grew louder and swirled around his ears; They even threw in a sickly sweet smell that made him choke while the laser lights bombarded him so fast his arms grew numb from hitting them. Now he could no longer touch the lasers with a fingertip; they were hitting him too rapidly for him to be that accurate. He had to bat at the lasers with both palms, increasing his area of contact, because, in spite of his extraordinary natural speed and precision, the laser points were coming faster than a human being could move. A small part of his mind wondered whether They would declare it illegal for him to use the palms of both hands at once, but he heard no warning buzzer. Anyway, They were the ones breaking the rules with too many colors, and that sweet stink. The lasers kept flaring, hundreds of them, faster and faster. Just when he thought his arms would drop off from fatigue, the bell sounded.

"Splendid, Corgan!" Mendor declared. Mendor had a face now, his Father Figure face, and it spread into a wide smile. "You have never played better! You didn't miss one—did you know that?"

Corgan shook his aching head. His score flashed in front of his eyes. 126,392. EXCELLENT WORK, CORGAN.

Flushed with victory, dizzy with success, he realized what that meant. No one in the Western Hemisphere Federation had ever earned a score that high. Corgan knew he could make a demand now. It was even expected of him. "I want something!" he declared.

Mendor slowly turned into Mother Figure. "Of course. Our wonderful champion deserves a reward," she said. Love, pride, approval—all of them radiated from her, washing over Corgan in a wave of maternal admiration. "What would you like?" she asked. "We're already bringing your favorite lunch—a steak."

"Real meat or synthetic?" he asked.

"A real steak from the Federation's famous cattle husbandry division. Do you know what an honor

13

that is, Corgan? The members of the Supreme Council are really pleased with you. They're willing to forget that you lost at Go-ball this morning."

"But I want something else," he demanded, his voice catching just a little. It was always dangerous to demand, never knowing where the line might be drawn.

"What would that be?" Mendor asked, still sounding like the Mother Figure, still indulgent. "What does our hero really want?"

"I want to see Sharla."

Mendor's image smeared. Her colors changed rapidly: red, pale green, purple, black, in swirls like spilled oil. Her face hardened and became androgynous, half Mother, half Father. "Don't push too hard, Corgan," he/she said.

"Bring Sharla out of Reprimand and let me see her," Corgan demanded. He tried to sound forceful, but he wasn't sure this was going to work.

"Eat lunch first," Mendor said curtly.

First? First means there might be a second, Corgan thought. Are They really going to let me see her?

But the rest of the day passed, and Sharla didn't appear.

Instead, Corgan had to spend the afternoon on Precision and Sensitivity training.

Two

The next morning, Mendor the Father Figure paced back and forth, back and forth, inside Corgan's Box. Four meters in one direction, turn around, four meters in the other direction, with his hands clasped behind him in his professor's pose. Of course it wasn't anywhere close to four meters he was pacing, because Corgan's Box was only two and a half meters wide. But the Box could create illusions of distance up to fifty meters long without any distortion. Beyond fifty meters the distortion started small but grew exponentially with each—

"Corgan, are you paying attention?" Mendor barked.

Corgan straightened himself. In the past five minutes, he hadn't heard a thing Mendor had said.

"You need a certain knowledge of history or you won't understand why this War is so important," Mendor scolded. "How much did you miss? What was the last thing you heard me say?"

No sense trying to fake it. "Uh . . . I guess . . ." Corgan searched his memory for the part he'd been paying attention to before his mind wandered. "I remember a picture of bodies all stacked together, wrapped in white cloth. . . ."

Mendor sighed. "That was Zaire—the Ebola epidemic. When they still bothered to bury the dead. Did you understand what I told you about Africa? That life could no longer exist on that continent after the year 2037? That the remaining Africans, the ones who had somehow survived the plagues, were divided among the other confederations. . . ."

Glad that he remembered *something*, so Mendor wouldn't think he'd daydreamed through the whole lesson, Corgan broke in, "Right. About a hundred thousand Africans went to live in the Eurasian Alliance, about half a million went to the Western Hemisphere Federation, and the rest to the Pan Pacific Coalition."

"Very good! Why did none go to the Middle East, Corgan?"

"Because that was where the nuclear war started."

"Correct. And how many died in the nuclear war?"

"Uh . . ." That part of the lecture must have been where Corgan's attention drifted. "Two and a half billion people?"

"Wrong! Only four hundred thousand actually died from the limited nuclear bombing. The other two billion died afterward, from radiation poisoning caused by the next two Chernobyl accidents."

"And then," Corgan began, wanting to redeem himself, "in the twenty years after that, three billion more people died from AIDS, Ebola, dengue fever, hanta virus—"

"—and Earth's surface became so contaminated that no one could survive except in domed cities," Mendor concluded. "Like the one we're living in."

Corgan intertwined his fingers and stretched, pulling his knuckles. "Mendor, there's something I want to ask you—"

"Why are you doing that to your hands?" Mendor interrupted. "Do they hurt? Does your skin itch?"

"No, I'm fine. I was just wondering—"

"Anytime you have the tiniest pain or ache, especially in your hands," Mendor ordered, "you're to report it immediately. You understand that."

"Yes, Mendor, how could I forget it? You tell me at least forty times a day."

"Don't exaggerate. What's the question?"

"Where are we?"

Mendor's image dimmed for a moment. He stopped pacing and lost his body, becoming nothing but a face that looked directly at Corgan, a face with several layers edged in different pale colors. "Where do you think? We're right here in your Box, Corgan."

"No, I mean, you said all Earth people who are

still alive live in domed cities. So where is our domed city?"

Mendor's image froze. For about six and thirteen hundredths seconds it remained unmoving.

He's gone to consult with Them about how much I can know, Corgan realized. Corgan hadn't thought the question was *that* major—not so important that Mendor would need to call a conference before he could answer it.

Mendor's face came alive again. "All right. If you want to know, pay attention." The Box filled with the image of a three-dimensional sphere that rotated to show oceans and continents. "This is Earth," Mendor said. "This picture was taken from space long ago, when people called astronauts went up in spaceships that orbited Earth. The last satellites were launched around the year 2010; actually, seventy-seven of them got put into orbit. They were called the Iridium Array. After that, all space launches stopped, because no nation could afford them. Are you following this?"

Corgan nodded.

"Now, seventy years later, only five of the Iridium satellites are still operating," Mendor continued. "All the other space vehicles are gone— they wore out, fell apart, or burned up when they dropped too close to Earth. And that's why it takes so long to get data from outer space these days."

"Uh-huh." Corgan sighed. It took almost as long to get Mendor to answer a simple question.

When he was in his Father Professor mode, he blathered all over the place, going off in all kinds of directions before he finally got to the point.

"Okay, I know we live on Earth," Corgan interrupted. "I know we're part of the Western Hemisphere Federation. I know we're on the North American continent—you've told me all that before. But exactly *where* on the North American continent are we?"

The image of Earth zoomed to North America and kept zooming so fast that Corgan felt airborne. Over mountain peaks and wide valleys, across a river, a lake, waterfalls, trees, another mountain range with white snow on the peaks . . .

"Here!" Mendor announced as the image froze. "In the old days, before the Federation, this place was called Wyoming in the United States of America. This is where our Federation headquarters is located. This spot right here . . ." Again the image zoomed, but more slowly this time. ". . . is where you occupy your particular physical space, Corgan."

It was an aerial shot of a transparent dome. For a short time Corgan's viewpoint stayed motionless, as if he were suspended right over the center of the dome. He strained to see through the glass, or whatever substance the transparent sphere was made of, so he could discover what was inside, but reflections of clouds and sky blocked his view.

About two kilometers in diameter, the dome

was supported by six curved beams. The whole structure rested on a circle of solid walls ten meters high. A causeway, completely enclosed, extended from the domed structure to a broad, gray, flat-roofed, windowless building.

"Where? Show me the exact spot I'm in," Corgan said.

He saw a flash of intense red light at the center of the flat-roofed gray building, which appeared to be about a hundred meters square, although it could have been larger or smaller. In virtual images, proportions were often deceiving.

"You're right here. In the spot where the light is. Now, is that sufficient?" Mendor demanded.

"No. Back off so I can see what's around us."

Again, moving slowly, the image pulled backward to reveal a paved runway on one side of the domed city. Two Harrier jet airplanes sat in front of a cylindrical hangar. As the view reverse-zoomed even farther, Corgan noticed a river curving around the expanse of land where all the buildings stood. Beyond the river grew a thick forest of cone-shaped trees that Corgan didn't know the name of.

"Why'd the Supreme Council pick here?" he asked.

"Energy. Solar power, wind power, water power, thermal power. Enough natural energy to keep this domed city running indefinitely. And the biggest reason of all—the area wasn't nearly as contaminated as most other places. That made it easier to sterilize."

The image vanished. "All right, that's enough," Mendor declared. "I think you may have even learned a little bit today. It's time for reflex practice, then lunch, and after that there's a surprise for you."

"Surprise?" Corgan rose to his feet. He'd been sitting for so long that the shape of his body had molded into the aerogel. "Good or bad surprise?"

"You'll think it's good," Mendor said. "As for me, I'm not so sure."

Corgan tried to keep from smiling. If the surprise was something Mendor the Father Figure didn't think he should have, then Corgan was sure to like it. And since it sounded like the Council was giving him something nice, he'd give Them a present in return. During reflex practice he'd pull out all the stops and play at the absolute peak he was capable of. That ought to make Them happy.

They chose to test him on button-hits-per-second. His previous high score was thirteen hits per second with the four fingers of his right hand, twelve with the four fingers of his left hand, and nine with each thumb. Because Corgan could gauge time in hundredths of a second, he calculated that by shaving just six or seven milliseconds off each hit, he could set himself a new personal record.

Concentrating hard, he pictured the neural

impulses that started in his brain, then fired along his spinal cord and branched into the nerves in his upper arms, lower arms, and wrists. When the neural transmissions reached his fingertips, each tiny neuron would fire instantaneously in response to his commands. Corgan closed his eyes and visualized the sparks traveling along each nerve path. In his imagination he magnified the synapses, picturing them in full color, in full motion, in 3-D. He took a breath, recited the pledge to wage the War with honor and so on, then said, "I'm ready."

As it turned out, he didn't even need to break a sweat. His time-splitting ability kept him aware of his score even while he reacted to the voiced instructions: "Third finger left, right thumb, index finger right, fourth finger left . . ."

Mendor was ecstatic. "You've set another Federation record!" he/she crowed. "That's two new records in two consecutive days."

"Good! Let's eat."

"Corgan, dear boy—"

"Lunch, please. Now!"

The meal was nothing more than synthetic meat and tasteless hydroponic vegetables, but Corgan hardly noticed. He wolfed it down, not because he was hungry, but because he wanted it to be over quickly so he could find out what the surprise was. Mendor the Mother Figure hovered over him, pointing out each little lapse in his table manners, making him finish every tiny bit of food on his plate, stalling on purpose.

"All right!" Corgan threw down his napkin. "I'm done. What's the surprise?"

Mendor sniffed. "*They* can show you. It was *Their* idea to call it a surprise."

Corgan waited for the Supreme Council to appear on the surround-image inside his Box. Slowly, the visualization appeared before him: a long table, with six faceless humans in uniform sitting at the table, staring at Corgan with shaded eyes. In the center of the six was an empty chair.

"Corgan!" The voice came from the second faceless one on the left. "You've done extremely well. We're pleased." The other five faceless ones murmured agreement, causing light waves to shimmer where Their mouths should have been if Their mouths had been visible.

"You knew from the start," a Councillor with an echo-chamber voice said, "that you would have two partners in the War. You, Corgan, are the team leader. You are the one who will be physically involved in the War. But your team also requires a strategist and a cryptanalyst—a code breaker."

"Yes, sir . . . ma'am." Corgan couldn't tell from the voice whether the speaker was a woman or a man.

"We're ready for you to meet your cryptanalyst."

"Is that the surprise?" Corgan asked. Why

would Mendor be all bent out of shape over that?

"It is. And here she is. Sharla."

The image of a girl appeared in the center chair. Sharla? This was not the beautiful Sharla who'd beat him at Go-ball. At least he didn't think so. He couldn't get a good look at her because her face was blurred. Frowning, squinting, Corgan tried to bring her image into focus, but it was as if several veils of light had been layered one over the other, slightly out of alignment.

"Hello, Corgan," she said.

Only the eyes looked like the earlier Sharla—they were blue and brimming with energy.

"Hi," he answered.

"Sharla is the most ingenious code breaker in the history of cryptology," one of Them said.

"I'm pretty good at Go-ball, too," Sharla remarked. Even though her image stayed out of focus, Corgan could tell she was smiling.

The six of Them buzzed disapprovingly. "Be serious, Sharla," one of Them said. "The War is only seventeen days away."

"Sorry!" Sharla ducked her head, but not before Corgan noticed that her eyes didn't look at all sorry. He felt a slight tug of disappointment that he couldn't see the rest of her any better, and wondered why the Supreme Council was bothering to blur her image. Just because Corgan had acted foolish over her yesterday?

"When do I meet the third member of my team?" he asked.

"Eventually. Soon," one of Them answered. Corgan had given up trying to figure out which one was talking. It was too hard to notice the slight wave motion where their mouths were supposed to be. "For today, we want you to become acquainted with Sharla. The two of you must learn to work together smoothly. Raise your hand, Corgan. Touch Sharla's hand."

Why bother, Corgan thought, but he did what he was told. What good was it to touch a tactile simulation of someone's hand? They could manipulate the tactile sensors to make a hand touch feel any way They wanted it to. Sharla's hand touch felt cool and rough, but it wasn't real. It was as artificial as her image. He was much more interested in how she would look in real life, but he'd probably never find out. The Supreme Council could tamper with her appearance as much as They wanted to, making her look incredibly beautiful or clouding her features in mist, like They were doing now. They controlled all the virtual images.

They controlled everything.

Three

The next day they practiced together for the first time, Corgan and Sharla. She looked the same as she had the day before—out of focus. Corgan wondered where Sharla lived. In a Box like his? In the same domed city he lived in? In Wyoming, where the wind and sun and thermal pools made energy? She could be next door or anywhere on Earth; in the virtual world, it didn't matter.

Corgan had never before thought about where the space might be that a person actually occupied. Virtual contact was all he'd ever known—virtual images of playmates, of Mendor, of the pets he was allowed to sleep with at night when he settled down into the warm aerogel inside his Box, holding a puppy or a kitten that had molded itself, as he watched, out of the same soft aerogel he slept on. After the pet took shape, its virtual heart would beat beneath Corgan's fingertips and its virtual breath would warm his cheek as it huddled against him. But the puppy—or whatever pet he'd chosen that night—never shed hair or nipped fingers or made a mess. And it never grew or wore out, because it disappeared whenever he got tired of it.

"Recite the pledge, Corgan," Mendor instructed.

Corgan raised his hand to say, "I pledge to wage the War with courage, dedication, and honor," as he did before every practice session. Sharla seemed to be saying the pledge, too, but with her image so out of focus, it was hard to tell whether she was murmuring the same words Corgan spoke. He stared intently at her lips.

"Pay attention, Corgan," Mendor ordered. "You and Sharla will start out with a few easy exercises to warm up. We'll change trajectory codes ten times while you play the first game. Sharla will adjust the program each time the code is changed so you won't miss any hits. You can play Golden Bees to start, since you like that game so much."

At the end of the Golden Bees session, Corgan asked, "What happened? I thought the trajectory codes were supposed to change."

Sharla laughed—at least that much of her was the same. Her laugh sounded as full of delight and amusement as when she'd hit him on the head with the Go-ball.

"The codes did get changed," Mendor said dryly. "You just didn't notice, because Sharla calibrated and adjusted each one in about a tenth of a second. She's fast."

"I really wasn't trying as hard as I should

have," Sharla said apologetically. The mischief in her eyes contradicted her modest tone.

"You must always try to do your best work," Mendor ordered.

They practiced a few more times, and then Mendor told them, "The rules governing the Virtual War were agreed upon, after five years of negotiation, by the Western Hemisphere Federation, the Eurasian Alliance, and the Pan Pacific Coalition. If either one of you breaks a rule unintentionally—even though it's just through human error—the infraction will be recorded. If you commit three such errors, we lose the War."

Corgan nodded. He'd heard it all before.

"But if you *deliberately* break a rule—just once," Mendor went on, "it's all over. We lose."

"How are the judges going to know if it's intentional or not?" Sharla asked.

Why would she ask that? Corgan wondered. Surely They'd gone over that with her. Dozens of times.

Mendor looked perplexed, but he began to answer Sharla, going off in all directions, like he always did, to talk about every other possible topic that had anything at all to do with what she'd asked. Mendor could never get right down to the core of a question.

Corgan gazed off into the distance while Mendor rambled on. Suddenly a small image of Sharla's blurry face appeared just inches in front of his eyes. "Don't say anything!" the tiny image warned him. "Just listen. Your Mendor won't catch on that I'm doing this. I fixed the codes."

Corgan was about to answer her but something slammed hard against his mouth. "Shut up!" the Sharla image hissed. "Just listen! Tonight at eleven o'clock I'll alter the codes so you can come out of your Box and They won't know. Meet me in the tunnel."

Corgan's eyes widened. It was a good thing Mendor wasn't focusing on him right then.

"Okay?" the Sharla image whispered. "If it's okay, blink real fast right now."

Corgan blinked.

"We'll meet person to person," the tiny face of Sharla told him. "Real. Not virtual." The image disappeared.

"You should be paying attention to this, too, Corgan," Mendor said irritably. "Or do you think you already know it?"

"Yes, I already know it," he answered.

"That kind of overconfidence could lead to serious mistakes," Mendor said. "Even if you think you know everything, it doesn't hurt to learn it over again."

"Sorry, Mendor," Corgan said. His voice shook a little. Mendor would think the quaver came from shame at being scolded. Let him think that. The real tremor was inside Corgan's chest, not his throat.

Did Sharla mean it? Could she do what she said—arrange it so they'd actually come face to face, and Corgan would be in the presence of *another human being* of bone and blood and muscle? He wondered if he'd have the courage to touch her, to take her hand.

What about infection? From the moment of his birth in the laboratory he'd lived inside a Box, away from any possibility of contamination. The Earth's population was so sparse now—hardly more than two million people left on the whole planet—that none of the three global confederations *ever* let people be together in the same space. Or have actual physical contact with one another. At least not as far as Corgan knew. Everything, for everyone, had to be virtual—always. Everyone lived in his or her own Box, enveloped in aerogel, nurtured by it, comforted and sustained by it.

Aerogel, the miracle substance. Discovered eons ago, back in the 1930s, but not till a hundred years ago in the 1980s had scientists figured out how to use it. Aerogel, called "frozen smoke." Light as air, a super insulator that protected against heat or cold but couldn't be frozen itself and could tolerate temperatures as high as two thousand degrees Celsius. Made from long strands of silicon dioxide—common sand—linked together with pockets of air. Aerogel was 99.6% air.

In a Box lined with aerogel, a person could live his entire virtual life, because aerogel carried electronic signals. Mixed with metal ions, it became a virtual medium that delivered 3-D, wraparound images as well as sounds, smells, touch—everything but taste. That afternoon, as Corgan advanced through a dozen practice levels, his senses were reacting to signals sent through aerogel.

"Very good. That's enough drill for now," Mendor stated. "You need some physical exercise." Immediately Sharla vanished and Corgan's virtual surroundings changed into a running track—a circular dirt track with white lines marking the edges and sweet-smelling grass growing in the middle. Obediently, he started to run faster and faster around the track, and all the time he was still in his Box, running on a treadmill imbedded in the floor, not a dozen inches from where he'd spent the whole day.

Corgan's aerogel-filled Box was his whole world, safe, sanitized, and lighted by a virtual sun. It was his cocoon. The surrounding aerogel-coated walls put him, electronically, into any scene created for him. Nothing could harm him in his Box, nothing could disturb him. Except Sharla, who managed to disturb Corgan's thoughts quite a bit later that night as he squirmed inside his aerogel bed.

Usually Corgan would fall asleep right when he was supposed to. Every night at exactly ten o'clock, Mendor the Mother Figure would call out, "Sleepy time, Corgan!" in a sweet, silly, singsong voice, and Corgan would settle himself into the aerogel, which had been cooled by five degrees for nighttime comfort. Within minutes he'd sink into the light sleep that always preceded his dreams. Dreams of ocean waves, or of the huge dinosaurs and pterodactyls that he'd picked out to decorate the walls of his Box when he was little. Sometimes he'd dream of soaring over trees in a forest of tall ferns and flowering branches. But since the day he'd played Go-ball with Sharla, he'd dreamed of other kinds of trees. Palm trees.

That night, though, Corgan wouldn't let himself fall asleep. He yawned, loudly, for Mendor's benefit. "'Night, Mendor," he said. Then he waited, lying as still as possible, counting the tiny grains of time as they cascaded over the sharp edge of his wakefulness. Since his sleep was always monitored by sensors embedded in the aerogel, he was afraid to move much—if he tossed and turned, as his body urged him to do, They'd check on him to discover what was keeping him awake: did he have a fever; did his hands hurt; did his throat feel sore?

"You're such a wonderful sleeper!" Corgan had been told over and over again when he was a little boy, as though sleeping were a skill as important as his ability to tell time to the hundredth of a second, or to throw a ball through a hoop thirty meters away, which he'd mastered before he turned three.

It is now twenty-two hours and forty-seven minutes and thirteen and eight-tenths seconds past midnight, he counted in his head. At twenty-two hours, fifty-nine minutes, and forty-five seconds he would stand up and attempt to walk through the door of his Box. What would happen? Could Sharla really fix the code so no one would know, so Mendor the Mother Figure wouldn't appear the instant Corgan stood up, asking him what was wrong—did he have to go to the Clean Room, had something upset him, did he feel too warm, and on and on and on?

He stood. Nothing, no Mendor. He moved through the pliable aerogel to the door of his Box. It opened. He stepped into the tunnel.

It was dark. Sharla must not have known how to light the passageway. Or else she was afraid to because They would notice light where it wasn't supposed to be.

"Corgan?" The whisper made a chill rush over his skin.

"Where are you?" he whispered.

"In front of you. Reach out."

It was going to happen, then. For the first time in his life, Corgan was going to touch a human being. He knew it would be dangerous, because contamination got spread by touch from person to person, which was why 93 percent of the Earth's human population had ceased to exist in the past eighty years. He'd been taught the danger ever since he could remember knowing anything, and now—he didn't care.

She touched him first. When her fingers reached his chest he trembled so violently that he almost fell against the wall—only his natural agility let him straighten himself in time.

"It's all right," she said softly. "Hasn't anyone ever touched you before?"

"No. What about you?"

Even muted, her laugh sounded joyful. "Corgan, I was bred to break codes. And on my own, I figured out how to break rules. Practically from the day I could walk They couldn't control me. I've been everywhere. I know everything. All about you, and the world, and the War we're going to win for Them, and . . ."

"All about me?"

"Sure. You and I were bred in the same laboratory. I looked up the records to find out about you."

"What about me?"

The words coming out of him sounded ordinary and rational, even though inside he felt total chaos—in his brain, in the pounding of his heart, in the way his breath kept catching in his lungs. *He was standing beside a living human being.* Except for that one fleeting brush of her fingers across his chest, they hadn't touched again. But he could feel her breath on his face when she spoke, still in whispers.

"You're one of Their greatest successes, Corgan," she said. "You were genetically engineered to have the fastest reflexes possible in a human. You and I happened to be in the same crop of genetic experiments, and the scientists almost went crazy when we were born. Because both of us turned out even better than they'd expected. We're not only superior, we're supreme. And I speak in all modesty. . . ." She laughed softly.

Her nearness made him dizzy. "What about the rest of the crop we were in?" he asked.

"Failures. The rest were all Mutants. Fourteen of them. Twelve died, and two went into the Mutant Pen. Since then, though, the geneticists have gotten better at it."

"How?" he asked, as softly as possible. If she had to lean forward to hear him, she'd be close enough that he could breathe the scent of her.

"The geneticists studied you and me to figure out what made us so good. It took a lot of years, but they've finally got a few more successes like us coming along, except those kids are all a lot younger than we are. Which is why you and I will fight the War."

The meaning of her words suddenly penetrated. Although still intensely aware of her presence, Corgan began to focus on what she was telling him. All of it was new to him. "Why didn't They teach me this?" he asked, forgetting to whisper.

"NNTK. No Need To Know. They might have

told you, if you'd ever bothered to ask, but I guess you never did."

Corgan rubbed his arms. The tunnel was cold.

"I know you're a time genius, Corgan, so how long have we been out here?" Sharla asked.

"Thirteen minutes, fourteen and fifty-six hundredths seconds. That's how long it was when you asked, but whenever I count in hundredths of second, by the time I say the words—"

"Better get back in your Box soon," she interrupted. "You're lucky you have a nice warm Box to live in."

"Everyone lives in a nice Box," he said.

"No they don't," she told him, sounding impatient. "They want you to believe it's true, but it isn't. Most people live in cramped dormitories. You've been raised in a Box because you're special. I am, too, but I learned how to get out and navigate the city when I was eight years old, and They never knew. They still don't know."

Corgan wanted to reach and touch her; instead he asked questions to keep her there. "What will happen if They find out you escape all the time?"

"Nothing. I'll go into Reprimand again, but what else can They do to me? They need me. I'm the best code breaker that ever lived. I'm the best by about a factor of ten."

She was either incredibly brave or incredibly foolish. "What about contamination?" he demanded.

"Won't you get infected if you keep leaving your Box?"

"The whole city is pretty much infection free," she answered. "The Supreme Council keeps scaring you about contamination because They want to you to stay isolated."

She's got to be wrong, Corgan thought. At least about that part of it. He wished he could challenge her on it, but they were running out of time.

"You'd better go—you don't want to get caught on your first time out," she said.

"First? Are we going to do this again?"

"Do you want to?"

"*Yes!*" Even though he remembered to whisper, the fervor in his voice echoed off the steel walls of the tunnel.

"Okay. Tomorrow night. Same time." Her fingertips grazed his cheek.

Not till he was back in his Box trying to settle himself in the aerogel did Corgan realize he'd never even seen her. Was she the beautiful Sharla he'd first met under the palm trees, or was she something else?

Four

"This is the land the War will be fought over," Mendor announced. "The Isles of Hiva."

The name meant nothing to Corgan. Tired, because he hadn't slept much the night before, he slumped into his aerogel as Mendor droned on about the Isles' location: between 7 degrees 50 minutes and 10 degrees 35 minutes south latitude, and between 138 degrees 25 minutes and 140 degrees 50 minutes west longitude. In the Central Pacific.

Slowly, the virtual re-creation of the Isles of Hiva filled the space around him, and Corgan came wide awake. Ocean waves splashed against rocky shores. The smooth circular trunks of palm trees rose high into canopies of flat, spiny fronds. Birds soared overhead and launched themselves into the water to spear fish. A warm, humid breeze skimmed Corgan's skin. The thunder of surf felt like heartbeats.

"Twenty volcanic islands forming two main groups . . ." Mendor the Father Professor's soliloquy continued, boring and lifeless. How could Mendor talk about something so beautiful and make it so dull, Corgan wondered. Was Sharla seeing and hearing this? She probably knew all about the Isles of Hiva. She'd probably broken into the code and discovered them for herself.

"A hundred years ago, seven thousand people lived on these islands," Mendor went on. "Fifty years ago, they all died in an epidemic of pakoko. That's what the natives called a particularly rapid-spreading form of tuberculosis."

"Then why are we fighting to win the islands if they're contaminated?" Corgan asked.

Mendor's color changed; it grew softer. "I'm glad you're interested enough to finally ask a question," he told Corgan. "Because amazingly enough, the islands are no longer contaminated."

"How'd that happen?" Corgan asked. He didn't really care so much about the answer; sometimes he just kept asking questions because it made Mendor happy. He felt guilty about what he'd done last night—sneaking out of his Box. If he pretended, now, to be really interested in the lecture, it might quiet his own conscience.

Mendor's image grew even brighter with pleasure. "As you know, Corgan, five satellites still orbit the Earth to send back—"

"Yes, I know."

"In 2073, scientists put together twenty years' worth of data they'd gathered about the

Isles of Hiva. It was discovered that the contamination was gone. A submarine party of robots landed there to confirm the data."

Corgan lifted his hand to feel the soft virtual breeze. Mendor went on, "Why have the islands become danger free? No one is certain. Perhaps because for a dozen years in a row, they received excessive rainfall—a hundred inches each year. That might have washed them clean and swept all the pakoko bacteria into the cold ocean current that flows north from the Antarctic, past the islands. Then the cold current might have killed the bacteria. Whatever the reason, the islands are safe for people to live on again."

Now Corgan really was interested. "You said the scientists figured this out in 2073. This is 2080. Why'd They wait so long to have a War over these islands?"

Mendor became a pulsing fount of radiant androgynous light. "Because of *you*, Corgan! For all these years the Supreme Council has used every excuse They could think of to delay this War. They stalled Their negotiations with the other confederations. They wrangled over rules and details. They demanded additional meetings and procrastinated at those meetings until it became embarrassing. All because of *you*. They were waiting for you to grow up, Corgan. Waiting for your skills to peak. And it's happened! Your abilities go far beyond anything ever measured before." Mendor's light dimmed a bit. "Sharla's, too, of course."

There were so many things he wanted to ask her. Things he could never ask Mendor. What was the Mutant Pen she'd mentioned? He'd never heard of it. What was it like in Reprimand? Why did she take so many chances?

But when they met in the tunnel that night he forgot all his questions. Sharla had brought a light.

"It's not very bright—it's just a piezoelectric stone. You squeeze this clamp on it and the stone glows for a second. I wanted to get a look at you," she said.

The stone measured only three centimeters wide on each side. "Let me," he said, taking it from her. "My fingers are strong."

The more pressure he exerted on the clamp holding the stone, the brighter the glow. Still, the piece was too small to cast much light. He was able to see Sharla more clearly than her blurred image at the War games practices, but not as well, in the dimness, as he would have liked. He saw that her hair was shorter than on the Go-ball court, yet it looked more golden. And her mouth! For a long moment he let the light shine on it. No virtual image could ever do justice to those full, moist lips.

"Better let the stone go out before They come snooping," she told him.

They stood together in the dark, with Corgan resisting the urge to reach out to her, feeling awkward because he ought to be saying something and he didn't know what to say. When two people were connected in the virtual world, conversation was easy. But here, with Sharla only inches from him, Corgan became tongue-tied.

"Uh . . ." All he could think of were the fractions of seconds being wasted while he stood there, as dumb as the stone in his hand. "Uh . . . what about me? Do I look the same as in my virtual image?"

"Exactly the same. No surprises."

Corgan's ears started ringing from the flood of sensations coursing through him, from the novelty of not only standing beside another human being, but this time, being able to actually see her. *Talk!* he commanded himself. A hundred phrases darted into his brain but shriveled there. *What should he say?*

Sharla took over. "Do you know that tomorrow we're scheduled to meet our Strategist?" she asked him. "Virtually. Right before lunch. And tomorrow night, I'm going to bring him here with me. If you want to meet me here again."

"Tomorrow?" A few seconds passed before Corgan nodded, hurt because she intended to let a stranger come with her the next time. Just when he was trying so hard to know her, to know how to act around her. He realized she couldn't see him nod in the dark, so he mumbled, "Yeah, I guess it's all right." Then he thought, Wait! Is she going to think I'm not anxious to meet *her*? "I mean, it's more than all right with me for us to meet again," he stammered. "I mean, you and me. And I guess it's all right if you bring him along. The Strategist. Do you have to?"

"Look, he's just a little kid," Sharla said. "Only ten years old."

"Then what's he doing on our team? Why would They put a ten-year-old with us to fight the War? That's crazy!"

She rested her hand on his arm. "This kid's a real prodigy. His name's Brig. I've seen him in real life. When They show him to you virtually, he'll look like an ordinary boy. But wait till you meet him tomorrow night."

It was a strange feeling—trying to push down his resentment over some ten-year-old intruder at the same time his blood raced because her hand was on his arm. The brand-new sensation of human touch: he wanted it never to end. Who cared what this Brig looked like? As long as Corgan and Sharla could stand together in the tunnel, Brig could look like one of those bodies consumed by flesh-eating bacteria, for all Corgan cared. Mendor had shown him images of those bodies, once, to convince him how important the coming War would be. "Safe, uncontaminated land is the most precious commodity on Earth," Mendor had said.

"Do you understand? Contamination has almost killed off the human race."

"What if the kid's infectious?" Corgan asked now.

Her laughter escaped before she could cover her mouth with her hands to stifle it. "Corgan, you really are funny," she whispered. "Brig won't be any more infectious than I am."

Stumbling over the words, he asked, "Could you put your hand back on my arm? I like it when you do that."

"Even if my hand has germs? Tell you what—how 'bout if I really contaminate you." She reached up in the dark and brushed his lips with hers. "That's called a kiss, in case you don't know. Remember it, because I won't do it again. From tomorrow on, we won't be alone anymore. Brig will be with us."

Corgan had never met Brig but he already hated him. "Then do it once more. Right now," he demanded.

"*Shhhh.* They'll hear you, and we'll both be in trouble."

"Would you like to hear how loud I can *really* yell?" he asked her. Then he said, "I'm sorry. I—I don't know why I said that. It's just that I've never been out of my Box before these last two nights with you, and I don't want it to stop, and this stupid clock keeps ticking in my head, eating up the time. . . ."

He felt her lips touch his face again, but this time, they lingered against his own lips a little longer—four and thirty-seven hundredths of a second.

"Good night," she whispered. "Till tomorrow."

"Did you brush your teeth?" Mendor the Mother Figure asked.

"Yes, I brushed my teeth," Corgan shouted. "I always brush my teeth. I always do what I'm supposed to, don't I?"

"What's the matter with you today, Corgan?" Mendor wondered. "Why are you so grouchy?"

"Because it was a stupid question you asked me. You had to know I brushed my teeth because you know everything I do—I'm monitored every second of my life. Even in the Clean Room."

That was not something Sharla had told him last night in the dark. It was something he'd figured out for himself as he lay awake, tossing and turning, remembering that kiss, not caring if his restlessness made all the sensors go off to alert Mendor.

Now Mendor's image changed through several shades of green.

"I'm sorry," Corgan told her. "I guess I'm starting to worry about the War. I think I need more practice sessions with Sharla." He was twisting the truth, and he felt a moment of guilt. But the

Supreme Council lied to *him* all the time, didn't They? Making him think everyone lived in a Box, like he did.

"If that's all that's bothering you, we'll increase your practice time," Mendor said. "It's good for you to be conscientious, Corgan, but you don't need to worry. Judging from what our surveillance teams have learned about your competition, your skills are infinitely superior to theirs. There, I probably shouldn't have told you that because They don't want you to become overconfident. But you shouldn't become *under*confident either. Now, why don't you relax a little before the first practice session? Do you want me to turn on Ocean Waves?"

"No. Not now." Corgan realized he still sounded like a cranky child. He softened his voice and asked, "Could I please have the Isles of Hiva, Mendor? All of it—image, sound, smell, touch . . ."

Mendor turned pink with pleasure. "Splendid!" she said. "The more you learn about the Isles, the more you'll understand our need to win them in a bloodless War. Naturally, the other confederations want the Isles, too. . . ."

Corgan breathed deeply. The smell of salt water reached him, carried on the island breeze. "Mendor, when you say 'bloodless War,' does that mean there once was a war with blood?" he asked. "I mean, people actually bleeding?"

Mendor hovered halfway between Mother Figure and Father Professor: If Corgan started to ask hard questions, Father would probably take over. "Even as little as a century ago, people killed each other in wars," he/she said.

"Yes, I know about nuclear bombs. But they didn't make people bleed, did they? They just gave people radiation sickness, and that's how they died." Corgan's attention was caught by a funny little creature with a shell and spindly legs. In the simulation, it skittered sideways across the beach. Corgan reached out a finger, but the creature dug into the sand and disappeared.

Mendor the Mother Figure was still talking. "Corgan, I realize that you're growing up and you want to know more about Earth's past, but we should wait until after the War," she said soothingly. "Don't clutter your mind now with unnecessary details. After you win the War for us, I'll answer anything you want to ask me. I promise!" When Corgan slumped in mild disappointment, Mendor added, "Just be glad you live in a time when wars are fought virtually."

The morning dragged as Corgan practiced alone. For two hours Mendor made him do P and S drills. In Precision and Sensitivity training, Corgan had to bring his hand as close as possible to a square of laser light without actually touching it. He couldn't determine his closeness visually; he had to use the nerve endings in his palms and fingers to feel the strength of an electromagnetic field between his hand and the image.

From ten millimeters away, he couldn't feel anything. Within one millimeter of the laser square, he would barely begin to sense energy. At five hundred microns from the image, the surface of his skin could perceive a tiny magnetic sensation. At two hundred and seventy microns, a slight tingle.

P and S workouts were the most difficult part of Corgan's training, and the most important part, Mendor said, although Corgan didn't know why. He'd practiced for two full years before he could turn the energy of electromagnetism into movement. It required all his concentration to bring his hands to within two hundred microns of a laser image—a distance the width of a delicate strand of a spider's web—and still not touch it. But when he learned to do that, he could make the laser image move. By itself.

Only half a dozen people in the whole world—at least as far as the Council knew—had control as precise as Corgan's. Because of it, he was favored, indulged, and given privileges that no one else got. On the down side, he was watched over and guarded every second of his life, day and night.

"Can I quit now, Mendor?" he asked after exactly two hours.

"Yes. Sharla's here, ready to practice with you."

It was the virtual Sharla, still unfocused. Doesn't matter at all, Corgan thought, because I know how she really looks. They can make her as blurry as They want, but I've seen the real Sharla.

"Recite the pledge," Mendor instructed them. Since Corgan had to repeat the pledge before every single practice session—sometimes as often as five times a day—he said the words automatically and never thought about what they meant. Now he stared at Sharla's out-of-focus mouth, trying to decipher whether she was saying the same pledge or something different. He couldn't tell.

"Ready?" Mendor asked. "Begin!"

They started with Triple Multiplex, a three-dimensional, three-layered maze that pitted artificial intelligence against Corgan's decision-making speed. He performed so well that Mendor heaped lavish praise on him, and Sharla smiled.

They had three more practices. Sharla needed to adjust the program to handle twenty-five switched codes, involving Corgan so intensely that he couldn't think of much else. He was sweating.

He asked Mendor, "Did you know we ran thirty-seven hundredths of a second over the time limit on that last game? If we do that in the War, we'll be penalized."

"Very good, Corgan. You caught that."

"Did you think I wouldn't notice?"

"Your proficiency was a bit off in the first game," Mendor said. "Not by much—just about three hundredths of a percent. Letting this last game run overtime by a fraction of a second was a little test They devised to make sure you were back on track. I told Them you'd be fine, and you were. Go to your Clean Room now and sanitize yourself. When you come back, you'll meet someone new."

Yeah, I know all about it, Corgan thought as moisture swirled around his naked body, as his hair got cleansed and his LiteSuit melted in the vapor before disappearing. He began to wonder—did everyone wear LiteSuits? For the sake of sanitation, these seamless suits of PVA—polyvinyl alcohol—were formulated to dissolve in water so they couldn't be worn more than once. But they were expensive; especially the kind Corgan wore, which reflected subtle highlights of color to match the wearer's mood. Sometimes he pretended to feel angry, then happy, then sad in rapid succession just to see how fast his LiteSuit could ripple with pale traces of gray or yellow or brown.

He'd have to ask Sharla if those people she talked about who lived in unsanitary dormitories got to wear LiteSuits. He'd ask her tonight. Except tonight, Brig would be with her. Ten years old! What kind of kid could be smart enough at the age of ten to plot strategy? And what was it about the way he looked? Sharla had hinted, but she hadn't really told Corgan anything except that Brig's virtual image would look a lot different from the way he was in real life.

When Corgan reentered his Box sixteen seconds late, the same faceless members of the Supreme Council were already there in virtual form, seated in the same straight line as before.

"Where's Sharla?" Corgan asked.

"She'll arrive later. After you meet your Strategist."

Brig's chair was in the middle of the row. Why did he need a chair anyway? Even real bodies didn't need chairs—aerogel let them sit suspended in comfort. And virtual bodies didn't need anything at all to hold them up because they were nothing but electronically transmitted impulses.

Except for his flaming red hair, Brig looked pretty ordinary. Corgan would never have guessed he was only ten. It was hard to tell what age he was supposed to be in the virtual image—not as old as Corgan and Sharla, but not especially young either.

"Corgan," one of the Councillors said. Corgan didn't bother to notice who was talking. "This young man will be your Strategist in the War. His name is Brig."

"Hi," Brig said. Corgan raised his hand in a small wave.

"You may be wondering, Corgan," another one of Them said, "why we've waited so long to introduce you to your two team members. Have you wondered?"

"Not really," Corgan answered.

Mendor suddenly appeared at the right shoulder of the Councillor who'd spoken last. "Corgan is an exceptional boy," Mendor said softly. "He rarely questions anything. He always does what's expected of him, no questions asked."

Corgan saw a tiny, scornful flicker cross Brig's eyes, and wanted to punch him in the mouth.

Another Councillor spoke. "Wise elders on the Council decided it would be best to bring the three of you to your highest skill level as individuals, before letting you practice together. Do you think that was a good idea, Corgan?"

He shrugged. "I guess."

Brig butted in. "Several conclusions could be drawn. Why waste valuable practice time when our abilities weren't yet at the peak of perfection? Now that they are—at least mine are—each practice will have greater value. Still, drawing on my instincts as a Strategist, I suspect the real reason hasn't yet been mentioned. My guess is that the War rules prohibited us from meeting before now."

Corgan's jaw dropped. The Council members laughed and congratulated Brig on his clever answer; some of Them even applauded.

Ten years old! The little toad talked like an old man of forty! Corgan said sarcastically, "Brilliant deduction, Brag. I mean Brig."

Mendor's image flared into all the colors of the rainbow. Corgan had embarrassed him.

In a chilly voice the Councillor said, "Corgan, the three of you are required to interact in cooperation and goodwill. No rudeness will be tolerated."

Corgan nodded, his cheeks flaming. He'd never before been rebuked in front of the whole Council.

Sharla appeared then, and Mendor the Father Figure announced, "You three will begin practice with an easy exercise and build to increasing levels of proficiency. Corgan, Brig, and Sharla. *As a team! Starting now.*"

Sharla, Corgan, and Brig the Mouth. Together for a whole afternoon. What fun.

Five

Eleven o'clock. Without even wondering whether Sharla had set the code, Corgan stepped out of his Box. Far down the tunnel, well past the door of his Clean Room, he saw a dim light flash on, then off. Sharla was signaling him to their meeting place, much farther along the tunnel than where they'd met before.

Moving silently, he reached her, took the piezoelectric stone from her hand and held it up to illuminate her face. "You came by yourself," he said. "I'm glad."

"I'm not alone," she answered. "Brig's here. Look down."

Startled, Corgan saw him. He was only half as tall as a ten-year-old should be and his head was twice as big. His arms and legs looked spindly. Even through the cloth of his LiteSuit, his torso appeared twisted.

Astonished, Corgan exclaimed, "You're a dwarf!"

"No I'm not! I'm a Mutant." Brig's real voice

was high and childish, much different than it had sounded that afternoon, when it must have been electronically altered to make him seem older.

"A Mutant!" Corgan had never seen one; he barely knew that such creatures existed.

Wobbling unsteadily on his twisted legs, Brig stared up at Corgan. In the dim light his features looked grotesque—bulging blue eyes, ridged forehead, ears that stuck straight out from his head through a great mop of flaming red hair. His nose was too big and his mouth too small, but as Corgan slowly took in Brig's appearance, he realized that shadows from the piezo light were exaggerating the boy's weirdness. "I thought all Mutants were . . . um . . . kind of retarded," Corgan said.

"Well, I'm a Mutant and I'm not the least bit retarded," Brig huffed. "You're right, though. Some of them are. Most of them are. Most of them die before they're seven. But here I am and I'm ten and I'm brilliant. A lot more brilliant than you are, Corgan-the-good-boy-who-never-questions-anything!"

"Don't be so prickly, Brig," Sharla chided him.

"Well, it's true. Corgan was bred for swift reflexes and incredibly precise control. But his brain barely hovers around genius level. Mine's *double* genius."

"And mine's *triple* genius, so back off, Brig," Sharla told him. "If you want to have a brain contest, you lose."

"Corgan loses worse," Brig muttered.

Sharla shook her head. "You can tell he's just ten," she said. "Still a big baby."

"The only thing big about him is his mouth," Corgan answered.

"Don't be nasty! You're worse than he is— you're older, so you ought to know better. Both of you better stop it right now or I'm leaving."

"No!" Corgan's hand shot out to stop her. "You promised me fifteen minutes, and there's still twelve left." If he had to put up with Brig to keep Sharla there in the tunnel, it was worth it. Fighting down his irritation, he said, "Sorry, Brig." Brig muttered, "Apology accepted." He reached up to put his hand into Corgan's. "Shake!"

The hand was so small! And warm. It filled only half of Corgan's palm, and felt as delicate and fragile as a hummingbird he'd once held, created for him to play with in the tactile simulator. Brig's fingertips twitched against Corgan's palm as if he knew Corgan could very easily crush him—fracture those frail, vulnerable, metacarpal bones—just by squeezing them in his own powerful fist. And Corgan could have. But Brig let his hand stay where it was until Corgan gave it an abrupt shake.

Sharla said, "I'm going to lift up Brig so we can all see each other's faces. You hold the stone, Corgan, to make enough light."

Brig's face did look less grotesque with the light shining directly on it, but Corgan wasn't looking at Brig. In the glow from the piezoelectric stone, Sharla reminded him of an electronic painting he'd once seen of a mother holding a child. A madonna. He sucked in his breath.

"What is it, Corgan? What's wrong?" Sharla asked.

"Just . . . the way you look. With him. I never got held that way when I was little. Not by a real person."

"Neither did I," she answered. "Only by robots." She paused, then said, "At least you had your Mendor, Corgan. Brig and I were raised by non-thinking robot caretakers."

"But not always. Not at first." Brig leaned his forehead against Sharla's cheek. "That's one advantage I had in being a Mutant. They put all the surviving Mutants together in a pen, like a litter of puppies. We could touch one another and crawl over each other, and some of the babies even sucked each other's thumbs. Robots took care of us, but we had the . . . the comfort, I guess you'd call it, of human touch. Even if some of the Mutants didn't look too human."

Brig twirled Sharla's hair with his spidery hand and said, "I spent six years in the Mutant Pen before They discovered how smart I was and took me out. So I got plenty of touching, like this. . . . Not to mention I got drooled on and slobbered over, too, 'cause that happened all the time in the Pen."

"Why are you so—I mean, you're right, it's easy to see you're intelligent, but—what made you look the way you look?" Corgan asked.

"I'm a case of genetic engineering gone wrong. Usually all the FLKs—"

"FLKs?" Sharla asked.

"Funny-Looking Kids. Actually, we were more than funny looking, we were flat-out weird. Usually kids like that are retarded, so that's why I was put into the Mutant Pen in the first place. But I'm different from the rest. I may be small and . . . and . . . deformed—" The last word was mumbled softly. Then Brig puffed out his scrawny chest to declare, "But I'm a *mental* giant!"

"Absolutely," Sharla agreed. "Corgan, how much time do we have left?"

"Two minutes and seven-some seconds. Listen, do we always have to stay out here in the tunnel? Could we go someplace else?"

"Where do you want to go?" she asked.

"To see some things. I've never seen anything in the real world. For a start, I'd like to see the Mutant Pen."

Angrily, Brig arched himself backward in Sharla's arms. "They're not a bunch of freaks for you to laugh at," he lashed out. "Mutants are people. It's hard enough for them without idiots like you coming to point at them and ridicule them."

"I would never do that!"

Sharla patted Brig's shoulder. "He really

wouldn't," she told Brig. "But if we do what you want, Corgan, I'll have to program your Box so you can be out of it for a whole hour. What if you get caught?"

"I'll take a chance."

"The practices went *reasonably* well today," Brig said the next night, "only we have to do better. The problem is obvious. Corgan, you just don't trust me."

Corgan didn't answer, because he couldn't deny it. The games were set up so that Sharla directly handled each code adjustment—it all took place between Sharla and the program, so Corgan rarely knew what she was doing.

Brig's role was different. Brig had to feed strategic decisions very fast into Corgan's mind through an auditory connector, with no time to explain why he'd made a certain choice. Corgan was supposed to act on Brig's input without hesitating. But each time, Corgan hesitated. And each fraction of a second counted against their score.

Maybe the Supreme Council members knew what They were doing when They made Brig's virtual image appear normal, made him look older than ten, and altered his voice so it didn't sound squeaky. Because Brig was right—Corgan really didn't trust him. That stunted, twisted, big-headed Funny-Looking Kid—how could anyone so weird be able to make good judgment calls?

Corgan didn't want to think about that now, not tonight. He was scheduled to have a whole hour with Sharla, and that was all that mattered. Even if Brig had to tag along.

"He can't walk like we do," Sharla said when they started out. "His legs are weak."

"I'll carry him," Corgan offered, although it was the last thing he wanted to do.

"No, Sharla will carry me," Brig said.

"How far is it?" Corgan asked.

She answered, "The Mutant Pen is too far for us to walk to, but there's something closer I think you'll be really interested in, so we'll stop there first."

"So pick me up, Sharla."

"I said *I'll* carry you." You little slug, Corgan added silently.

"No, no, no, no, no! I know who I want, and it's not you," Brig whined. "Sharla, carry me, pleeeease!"

"I can't believe you!" Corgan cried, barely able to keep his voice down. "Half the time you talk like some grown-up professor and the rest of the time you're a big crybaby!"

"Yeah, well, I'd rather be a paradox than an ape-armed troglodyte like you."

Frustrated, Corgan clamped his jaw shut so tightly his molars hurt. He was sure he'd been insulted, but how could he fight back when he didn't understand the words Brig used? Paradox? Troglodyte? He'd never heard them before.

"Are you two finished? Can we get on with it?" Sharla asked, picking up Brig. "Make sure you stay right behind me, Corgan. I know my way through these tunnels. Brig, you hum or something—but keep it low—so Corgan can follow the sound of your voice."

Oh great, Corgan thought. Now I have to listen to the little toad croaking in the dark. He decided to ignore Brig; there was no rule that he had to talk to him. "When you said it's too far to walk, Sharla—how else are we going to get there?" he asked, trying to stay right behind her without stepping on her heels.

She whispered, "Better not tell you now. These walls echo. Anyway, you'll find out soon."

The tunnel widened, and a small amount of light glowed in a thin strip set flat into the middle of the floor. "Okay, we're here at the first stop," Sharla murmured.

Corgan asked, "Where's here?"

"We're about a quarter way through the causeway that connects our building to the domed city. Brig, brace your legs. I'm going to set you down."

Corgan could barely make out Sharla in the darkness. She seemed to be holding something in one hand and tapping it with the index finger of her other hand. "What's that?" he asked.

"My code alteration device. There's a shielded window here, with a room behind it. I'm trying to realign the numbers and make the window transparent so we can see through it."

"Me too," Brig said. "I want to see. Pick me up again so I can see."

Gradually, like a steamy wall in Corgan's Clean Room when dry air hit it, a clear spot expanded in the seemingly solid panel in front of them. "Look in there," Sharla said. She picked up Brig. "See them?"

"People," Corgan answered. There were six of them, four men and two women. None of them was young; none of them looked especially out of the ordinary. One had lost most of his hair; one slumped in a chair as though he didn't have the energy to sit up straight; one of the women rubbed her temples as if her head hurt, and as she rubbed, her fingers pulled her eyes into ugly slits. The six of them talked listlessly. They seemed to interrupt each other a lot.

"Who are they?" Corgan asked.

"The Supreme Council."

"*What! No!*" Corgan remembered the way They'd looked in the virtual world—large, faceless, eyes hidden in shadow, erect bodies dressed in flawless uniforms with fluorescent medals.

"It's true," Sharla said. "There They are. Take a good look."

Corgan stared for a full minute. Then he asked, "In our meetings, why do They make Themselves look so—"

"Commanding? Mysterious?" Sharla finished. "Mind control. They don't want you to know They're just ordinary people who could maybe make mistakes."

"Why not?" Corgan asked.

"Because They don't trust people to handle truth. They have to make everything seem mystical so They can dictate to people. So people will do exactly what They tell them to. That's why They love you so much, Corgan, because you never question anything." She shifted Brig in her arms. "Seen enough?"

"Too much!" Corgan cried.

"Not so loud! If They hear a sound, They might look over this way and I'm not sure how opaque the wall is from inside." She set Brig on the floor. "Anyway, They're not such terrible people," she told Corgan. "They really want to do what's right for the Western Hemisphere Federation. The bad part is that They think They're the only ones who know what's right, for the Federation and everyone in it. And They're the ones that get to make the rules."

Corgan stared at the plain, unimpressive people beyond the wall. One of Them kept pinching his nostrils together and sniffing as if to stop a sneeze. A woman scratched the top of her head, then examined her fingernails.

"What are They doing there?" Corgan asked.

"Having a secret meeting. They come here

when They want to talk privately. They'd have fits if They knew I knew about this place."

The Supreme Council! Average-looking people who couldn't even keep Their hideaway secret from a fourteen-year-old girl. Disillusioned, Corgan turned away, and Sharla closed up the transparent circle. "On to the next stop," she said.

"The Mutant Pen?" Brig asked.

"That's the last stop. We're going to pass the hydroponic gardens on the way—I thought Corgan would like to know where his meals come from."

"Make sure you leave enough time for the Mutant Pen," Brig pleaded. "I want to see it again—it's been a long time."

They'd walked rapidly for six minutes forty-three and seventeen hundredths seconds when Sharla said, "Wait here. We have to take a hover car."

Corgan was about to ask what a hover car was, and how they could take one without anyone finding out what they were doing, but Sharla disappeared. After fourteen seconds she came into sight again, under a ceiling light. She was talking to a man who wore a dark one-piece outfit of heavy cloth, definitely not a LiteSuit. Five more seconds and she gestured for Corgan and Brig to join her.

"This is Jobe," she said, introducing the gray-suited man. "Jobe, I'm not going to tell you the names of these two guys. Just being safe, you know."

Jobe held out his hand for Corgan to shake, but Corgan couldn't make himself touch it. He'd barely overcome his fear of contamination enough to touch hands with Sharla and Brig. And Jobe's hand looked disgusting. Little cracks in the skin were ingrained with dirt, and the fingernails were rimmed with black grease. That thick, rough, filthy hand had to be crawling with bacteria.

"Well," Jobe said, grinning as he dropped his hand after a moment, "here's a hover car comin' along right now. It's not supposed to stop here, but I can maybe slow it down a little. You three will have to jump inside real fast. I'll flip up the dome when it gets close enough, and you can run alongside the car and hop over the side. Once you're in, I'll close the dome again. If you miss this one, you're out of luck. Okay?"

"Okay. Thanks, Jobe," Sharla said.

"So run!"

Corgan scooped up Brig into his arms as the hover car, moving silently only three centimeters above the floor, drew close to them. It followed the path of the dimly glowing magnetic strip in the floor. The car moved forward quickly, but neither Sharla nor Corgan had trouble keeping up with it. Sharla leaped over the side and reached for Brig.

By then the car had traveled into total darkness. Corgan kept his hand on the edge of the dome so he could feel where it was going.

"Hurry up!" Jobe cried, panting as he lumbered along beside them. "Jump in now. Fast!"

Corgan managed to clamber inside just before the dome slammed shut, grazing his knuckles.

"I hope I'm not bleeding," he said.

"Afraid of a little blood?" Brig mocked.

"No. Mendor will pester me about how I got my knuckles skinned, that's all." He slid back onto something hard. "These are real seats, aren't they?" he asked. "They're not aerogel."

"They're aerogel," Sharla answered. "Only they're rigid-molded, not flexible. They last longer that way."

He felt along the back of the seat until he touched Sharla's shoulder. She reached up to squeeze his hand. "Enjoying the ride?" she asked.

"How'd you arrange this?" he wondered.

"I know all the hover-car maintenance people. I don't need a whole lot of sleep, Corgan, so I prowl at night. And this whole city is too big to travel around on foot—we haven't even reached the domed part yet. But we're getting close. Right now we're still in the connecting causeway."

Brig burrowed backward, wedging himself between them as though he didn't want to be left out. "You are one very impressive contriver, Sharla," he told her. "How do you get the staff people to let you ride these hover cars?"

"Bribes," she answered.

Corgan said, "I don't know that word."

"It means I give them something, and they let me sneak on the cars."

"What do you give them?" he asked.

"Tips on the lottery. You know what a lottery is, don't you, Corgan?"

"Uh-huh. Sure." He really didn't, but he was tired of sounding ignorant.

"Since I was genetically engineered to be a code breaker," Sharla explained, "I'm also great at figuring the probability of numbers hitting in the lottery. I'm not right all the time, but enough that my tips give the guys a winning edge. I just told Jobe to play 716."

Corgan didn't have any idea what she was talking about.

"Is that legal?" Brig asked. "To give them tips?"

"Do you care?"

"No, but Corgan the Obedient probably cares." Brig's sharp little elbow dug into Corgan's ribs.

"It's the way I operate," Sharla said. "I was genetically engineered to calculate numbers. And somehow, I got this strong urge to take risks. Plus, I like to find out things. So I use my numbers genius to pay for the risks when I snoop around. It works great. Usually."

The hover car had come alongside a lighted area: a huge room filled with tables that held growing plants. Dozens of people, dressed in dark suits of heavy cloth like Jobe wore, walked between the tables. They talked to each other, and they stopped every few meters to examine leaves and spray mist on the plants. Farther along, others cut plants and dropped them into square aerogel boxes. Sometimes their hands touched. Apparently all of them breathed the same air. Didn't anyone in there worry about contamination?

"This is where your food comes from, guys," Sharla said.

Corgan asked, "What are they growing in there?"

"Soybeans, mostly. Just about everything we get fed, from turkey to toast, is really soybeans in disguise," she answered.

"I get real steak sometimes," Corgan told them, and instantly wished he hadn't said that.

Brig sneered, "Of course Corgan would get steak. Corgan, the darling of the Supreme Council. Corgan, the fabulous physical animal that gets favored and fussed over and fed real steak while Mutants like me get recycled garbage."

"Quit complaining," Sharla told him. "It's probably better for you anyway."

Corgan stretched to see better. "There's the dome!" he exclaimed. "The dome that covers the whole city! I've only seen it virtually before. And— *I can see through the dome! I can see real stars!*"

"Let me see, too!" Brig scrambled onto Corgan's lap. "Where? Show me! Lift me up! I haven't seen true stars since I was six, when they took me into the other building."

The hover car kept moving but the stars stayed still: tiny chips of cold light in the darkness outside. As they traveled the corridor that bisected the hydroponic gardens, both boys sat in silence, fascinated by the night sky. "Those stars look so much nicer than virtual ones," Brig murmured. "See there? That's Orion. I remember Orion. Doesn't he look great?"

Corgan nodded. "Really great." Without realizing it, he tightened his arm around Brig.

Six

Corgan was so enthralled by the night sky that he hadn't even glanced at Sharla for seven full minutes and thirty-two and a fraction seconds—not since the hover car had entered the domed, lighted area. He regretted it the instant he turned toward her.

Illumination from the hydroponic gardens gave him his first-ever look at her in a decent light. For once she was fully visible from head to toe, from her boots to her shining blond hair.

She turned and caught him staring at her. Embarrassed, Corgan stammered, "Uh . . . I was just wondering. About your hair—isn't it too long? I mean, it's really nice, but the rules say hair can't be longer than five centimeters. So why is yours—?"

"I told Them it's my hair and if I want to wear it long I will," she answered matter-of-factly.

She amazed him. Sharla seemed to break rules and suffer no consequences. How did she get away with it?

"I could look at these stars forever," Brig said, "but when do we get to the Mutant Pen?"

"Soon," Sharla answered.

Corgan kept watching her in the pale light. Suddenly it occurred to him that the same light must be making him visible, too, and not just to Brig and Sharla. "All those people working there in the gardens," he said, "can't they see us? I mean, the light from there is shining in here. On us."

"Don't worry. The car's bubble dome has a reflective coating on the outside. If the people in there bother to look up from their work, all they'll see is glare." She peered ahead. "Something's wrong, though, on the track about twenty meters in front of us."

"Get off my lap, Brig," Corgan said. "I need to look out."

He leaned forward, pressing his face close to the transparent bubble dome. "We're coming up on it pretty fast, whatever it is."

"It's another hover car," Brig announced. "Looks like it's stalled. See, it's not moving. It's just sitting there on the floor."

"Move, move, move, MOVE!" Sharla cried, clenching her fist.

"Who, me?" Brig asked.

"No, that car up ahead. Get out of our way!" she ordered, as if saying it would make it happen.

Brig braced himself. "Are we going to crash?"

"No, we can't crash. This car stops automatically if it comes within three meters of any obstruction. But I can't tell if there's another car in front of that one," Sharla said. "If there's a real jam-up and we get stuck here, we're in major trouble. Corgan, how much of our hour is left?"

"Twenty-three minutes, forty-seven seconds and . . ."

Their car came to a sudden halt, rocking them forward. "We've got to get out of here!" Sharla cried. "There's at least six stalled cars up ahead."

"Can't we just reverse this one?" Corgan asked.

"Hover cars only go in one direction. They loop," she told him. "Corgan, if we run from here back to our Boxes, how long will it take?"

"I don't know! I don't know how fast you can run, and Brig . . ."

"You'll have to carry him. Right now we need to get this bubble dome open so we can get out. See that handle on your side? Push it hard."

He pushed, but nothing happened.

"Harder!" she commanded.

Corgan pushed with both hands. Nothing.

"Okay!" She took out the small flat control box she'd used to make the wall turn transparent at the Supreme Council's meeting room. "I've got to figure the code that secures the latch. Lean back, guys. The beam has to focus straight on the door."

Her long thin fingers flew over the numbers on the control box. "I don't know what's wrong," she said through clenched teeth. "Either something's jamming the door or the whole hover-car system's down."

Corgan stayed quiet. This was outside his area of expertise. Sharla would have to handle it.

Desperately, she kept punching numbers. "I can't make it work!" she cried.

Corgan asked, "Do you want me to break out the bubble dome?"

"Yeah, right!" Brig scoffed. "You break it, and every security guard in the gardens and every mechanic in the whole transport system will be here in about ten seconds."

"Yeah, well, there's about nineteen minutes left right now before we're locked outside of our Boxes for the rest of the night," Corgan lashed back at him. "So come up with some other strategy, Double Genius Mouth-Off."

"Break the bubble dome, Corgan." Sharla sounded grim. "We're out of options. Just do it."

Corgan had no experience with molded aerogel. Regular aerogel, the kind that lined his Box, was too flexible to break, although with enough pressure it could be torn. All he could try to do now was smash the molded bubble dome with both arms and hope it would break outward, hope it wouldn't explode into fragments that could fly into their eyes and cut them.

"Here goes!" he said. He raised his arms chest high, with his fists together. In a burst of force he flung both fists outward against the dome. His first blow shattered it. All the pieces flew away from them in a spray of chips that caught the light like tiny stars.

"Get out!" Sharla picked up Brig, ready to hand him to Corgan as soon as Corgan climbed over the side.

"They'll see us!" Brig wailed. "It's light out there!"

Sharla hesitated. "You're right." Once more her fingers flew across the controller box. Suddenly everything went dark.

"Here, Corgan, take Brig," she said. "I'll lift him out to you."

Corgan heard a tearing sound and whispered, "What happened? Did someone get cut on the shards?"

"Just my LiteSuit. It's ripped," Brig answered. "Don't drop me, Corgan!"

"Go!" Sharla cried. "Corgan, follow that magnetic strip—it gives off a glow. Run back the way we came. Fast!"

"I'm gone." Even carrying Brig, Corgan could move faster than Sharla. She stayed behind him, close enough that he could hear her breath coming hard as her feet pounded the floor.

"How much time?" she panted.

"Eight minutes seven seconds."

"Go without me," she said. "You have to get Brig back to his Box first. Brig, can you tell Corgan how to get there?"

"I'm scared!" Brig whimpered.

"Can you tell Corgan how to get to your Box!"

"I guess so."

"That's not good enough!" Corgan hissed in his ear.

"YES! I'll tell you! But you probably won't listen to me anyhow," Brig whined. "You don't trust me."

"You crybaby! Do you want to get us all into trouble?" Corgan shook Brig in exasperation, but stopped shaking him because it broke the rhythm of his running stride, and anyway Brig really was starting to cry. "We're a team!" Corgan barked. "Act like a team!"

"Go on, pull ahead of me," Sharla said. "I know I'm holding you back. How many minutes left now?"

"Six minutes and twenty-eight and nineteen hundredths seconds."

"Dammit, Corgan, do you always have to be so exact? 'Six and a half minutes' would have been fine."

That was the last he heard from her. Sharla dropped back at the same time Corgan increased his speed. He felt exhilarated. He'd never before run in an open area. Always before he'd run on a treadmill on the floor of his Box, although it never looked like a treadmill: The virtual images that surrounded him made it appear he was on a sandy beach, or running along a forest path, or a mountain trail, or a racing track. Now his legs stretched almost straight out as they pumped faster and faster in a sprint. His balance adjusted easily to the slight weight of Brig in his arms.

"Turn! Turn!" Brig yelled. "Over that way!"

"Are you sure?"

"Do you think I don't know where my own Box is?"

"You didn't seem to know back there."

Corgan spun into the turn without losing momentum. He felt great! He'd never tried anything like this before: running at top speed on a real floor, carrying an awkward, lumpy weight, and yet being able to talk in whole sentences without even panting. He was stronger than he'd thought. Brig's skinny arms clamped Corgan's neck like a vise, but even with that little leech hanging on to him, Corgan ran like a champion. I'm the best! he thought.

"Here! Stop! This is it." Brig tried to leap from Corgan's arms and almost tumbled to the floor. Without as much as a thank-you he scurried into his Box, scrabbling like a scared rat.

"And good night to you, too, Big Brain," Corgan said. Then he turned and raced back along the passageway. He reached the fork where he should have angled toward his own Box, but he was enjoying himself so much he spun around and retraced his path, sprinting back in the direction of the abandoned hover car, just for the freedom of it.

And to see if Sharla might still be in the corridor. But she was gone. The clock ticking in his head told Corgan he had enough time to make it back to his Box and slide through the door with at least a tenth of a second left before Sharla's programming clicked the door shut. He laughed out loud.

Seven

"Where did you get that cut on your hand?" Mendor demanded.

Corgan had forgotten about his scrape from the hover car. He hadn't even noticed it during the morning sanitizing in his Clean Room.

"It's nothing," he said.

"Let me see!" The tactile simulator turned on and Mendor the Mother Figure reached out to grasp Corgan's hand. "How did this happen?"

"I don't know. Leave me alone!"

"Any little break in the skin can be dangerous," she said patiently. "Be a good boy, and—"

"*Stop it!*"

"My, we're a bit testy today, aren't we?" she crooned as tiny flashes of light went off over his scraped knuckles. He was being cauterized with laser beams. "Your hands are extremely important, Corgan. They must always be protected."

With a strong pull he yanked his hand free.

"Corgan!" It was Mendor the Stern Father now, glowering at him. "Since you seem to have no concern for your own safety, let me remind you what can happen. A microscopic bacteria called streptococcus pyogenes can invade your body through any chance opening in the skin. It can cause an infection known as necrotizing fasciitis, also called 'flesh-eating disease.'"

Mendor's image enlarged until his purple-gray face filled the Box. "If you get this disease and you're lucky enough to survive, Corgan, you may lose quantities of skin and fascia—the fibrous tissue surrounding your muscles. Then your gangrenous fingers and toes will be amputated. Would you like to see some of the victims?" Instantly, pictures of grotesque, dripping bodies filled the surround-scene, their lesions so repulsive Corgan threw his hands over his eyes.

"Turn it off!"

The images slowly faded as Mendor said, "Tell me, Corgan, you're a boy who was born with the fastest reflexes and the most unerring precision ever known to humankind. Just how would you play games if you had no fingers?"

Corgan shook his head.

"Now, Corgan, how did you get that broken skin on your hand?"

"Dammit, Mendor, I told you I don't know."

Mendor's gasp was like a gale blowing through the Box.

"Where did you learn that word, Corgan?"

"What word?" But he knew exactly the word Mendor meant.

"That swear word. Never in your entire life has that word been spoken in your presence. Where did you hear it?"

"From you. You said it—you just don't remember. Your internal programming must have some kind of a memory glitch. . . ." Corgan felt the sweat break out in his hands as the lies came out of his mouth.

"My programming is never faulty," Mendor hissed. "This time you really have gone too far, Corgan. You're lying! I have no choice but to send you to Reprimand."

Reprimand! Corgan's LiteSuit turned dark from apprehension. He had never been put into Reprimand—he'd never before had to be punished for wrongdoing. He couldn't even imagine what Reprimand would be like, except that it had to be something awful.

His ears filled with a staticky whirring that swelled and ebbed from loud to soft and back so rapidly that his head started to spin. Then he felt his whole body rotate, spiraling, whirling, pivoting, head up, head down, sideways. . . .

And there he was. In Reprimand. But it wasn't a place; it was simply total emptiness and almost total darkness and gloom. A feeling of despair swept through him, filling his heart, his whole body, and even his skin, down to each separate pore. He wanted to run, but couldn't move. He hung suspended, motionless, not sure whether he'd landed vertically, horizontally, or at any other angle up or down.

"Corgan! Corgan!" It might have been Mendor's voice he heard or the voices of the Supreme Council; it seemed he recognized all of them in the words. "We have given you everything. Isn't that true?"

He nodded, glad he was able to move his head, at least.

"From the time you were a tiny boy, we've done all we could think of to make you happy. Haven't we, Corgan?"

"Yes," he whispered.

"We gave you toys. Dinosaurs decorating your walls. And do you remember the koala bear, Corgan? You wanted a koala with blue eyes and soft fur, one that would chase a ball like a puppy. You named it—what did you name it, Corgan?"

"Named the bear Roland," he answered, the words like ribbons unwinding from his throat.

"Ah yes," the voices continued. "We had to create a special program to make Roland do all the things you wanted him to. We set our cleverest engineers to work on the project, and we told them, 'Don't worry about how much time it will take you to perfect it. Don't worry about expense. This toy is for Corgan.' They worked night and day to build Roland for you."

"I loved Roland." Tears stung Corgan's eyes as he remembered.

"For a little while," the voices murmured. "For only a little while you loved him. Then you stopped playing with him."

Now a whole additional chorus joined in to sigh, "We asked why you no longer played with Roland. And you said . . . you said . . . that Roland had bitten you. Do you remember that, Corgan? You told a lie."

Lie! Lie! Lie! The word echoed as if from a deep cavern.

Incredible, Corgan thought. They had to go all the way back to when I was six to find the last lie that I told.

"We didn't mind that you'd stopped playing with Roland," the voices lamented. "Even though we had put so much time and effort and scarce resources into that special koala that you wanted, and you only played with it for a few days—we were glad it made you happy. Even if just for a little while. We've always tried to make you happy, Corgan."

"Yes," he gasped. His throat felt like it was closing from the inside.

"But when you lied, Corgan . . ." Now the face of Mendor the Mother Figure wrapped around him, gray and furrowed, the surface sliding downward in despair. "You broke Mother's heart."

"And you wounded Father's pride." Slowly

Mendor the Father Figure appeared, somber and dark.

"I've been bad," Corgan whimpered, sounding like a six-year-old. He hadn't meant to say that—where had it come from? He cleared his throat, wondering why his voice had suddenly turned thin and high-pitched. Then he saw himself in the wraparound image: He *was* a six-year-old, with straight black hair falling in bangs over his forehead, with his mouth drawn down and his soft lips trembling.

"No . . . you're not a bad boy, Corgan," Mendor the Mother Figure said once again, as she'd said so many years before. "You're a very good boy. But you mustn't tell lies."

"I'm sorry! I won't tell lies ever again."

"We've always done everything we could to make you happy. We gave you everything you asked for. We gave you our trust. You must always tell us the truth, Corgan."

He said, "Yes," through trembling lips, not sure whether he was Corgan the six-year-old or Corgan the long-legged, strong-armed virtual champion. Discovering he could move his arms, he reached up to knead his throat, trying to get his real voice back.

"We trust you to do what is right."

There was nothing Corgan could safely reply. A faint chord of music, deep and dolorous, rumbled across the dark emptiness.

"Your happiness matters to us, Corgan, more

than anything." The words matched the tempo of the barely heard music, which built slow, heavy, minor chords into a song of infinite sadness. "Your happiness will always matter. Our love for you will never diminish. Even when you betray us." Betray! Betray! Betray! It hung in the air, vibrating.

"Honor, Corgan. Truth. These matter most. The trust between parents and son."

He didn't answer. Couldn't answer, because it was guilt, now, that rose into his throat. They were right. He'd told a lie. Lying was wrong.

"After all we've done for you, Corgan, can you give us just one thing in return?" The music throbbed softly, like a slow heartbeat.

"What's that?" he whispered. "What can I give you?" He knew what They were going to ask for.

"The truth, Corgan. All we want is that you tell us the truth."

"What truth?"

"A very small matter. So small! Just tell us— where did you hear that word you used this morning?"

"I can't remember."

The music grew louder, anguished. The space around Corgan seemed crowded with creatures, all of them weeping, pressing against him, smothering him, drowning him in their tears.

"Please, Corgan, try to remember. We don't blame you. You're the innocent one. Others have led you into error. We want desperately to believe in you again. We love you. Tell the truth, and all will be forgiven. All will be forgotten. Nothing will be held against you."

Shadows filled the darkness, moving shapes bent over in sorrow. The shapes hovered around him. Phantom hands reached up to touch him in supplication.

"Where did we fail, Corgan? What more can we give you? We gave you so much, but it wasn't enough!" The music grew louder; the weeping rose to a new level of anguish.

Corgan's tears rolled slowly down his cheeks. It was true; They'd always been good to him, and now he'd caused Them pain. Would it really matter if he admitted everything? He'd insist on taking full responsibility. They said he'd be forgiven.

"Once more, Corgan. Who spoke that word to you?"

"Sharla," he whispered.

"When?"

"Last night. I don't know!"

"Where?"

"In the corridor. Don't punish her!"

Light blinded him. He was back in his Box, with Mendor beside him.

"We will not speak of this again," Mendor the Father Figure thundered. "Ever! How many days remain before the War, Corgan?"

"Twelve."

"A full morning of practice has been lost because of this lie you told."

"It's only been a few minutes!"

"The matter must be pursued further. Be cautious from now on, Corgan. That is all I have to say to you."

Corgan sat up, wet from sweat and tears. His gut felt raw, and his ears rang. His Box filled with images of the Isles of Hiva—palm trees with their broad leaves waving in the wind, the surf rushing up on sand and then rolling back. So it was all supposed to be over, and They were trying to soothe him with Hiva while They—did what? Went after Sharla! And Brig, too, probably!

Corgan paced his Box. He'd been forgiven quickly enough, or at least he was out of Reprimand. So Sharla and Brig ought to be forgiven, too. After all, the three of them were in it together. The other two would probably be questioned in Reprimand just as he'd been. It hadn't been so bad, really. Yet, remembering it, his skin turned clammy. If nothing really terrible had been done to him, why did he feel so rotten?

He knew why. He'd betrayed the people he cared about. Not Mendor, not the Council. He'd betrayed Sharla and Brig.

A whole hour late, practice was about to begin.

"Where's Sharla?" Corgan asked.

She appeared, even more out of focus than

before. What a joke, Corgan thought, the way They make her look. Are you all right, he tried to ask her with his mind, but her eyes didn't respond.

"What about Brig? Where's Brig?" Corgan demanded.

"Brig is—not here. He won't practice with you today." Mendor spoke in a flat, unrevealing tone.

"Why?"

Mendor didn't answer.

The tiny image of Sharla's face appeared close to Corgan's eyes, as it had that one time before. "Keep quiet, don't say anything," the image told him. "Brig is still in Reprimand. They want him to tell why his LiteSuit got ripped, but he won't talk. He's really scared! They put me in Reprimand, too, but I'm used to it and I didn't admit anything."

Brig, that little crybaby, was holding out against Them? And Sharla hadn't admitted anything. Only Corgan had! He stood up halfway as the Sharla face vanished.

So! The Supreme Council wanted honor? Mendor wanted truth? Fine! He'd give Them truth.

He shouted, "Sharla, listen to me! I told Them wha—"

Inhumanly high-pitched shrieking hit his eardrums with such force he felt as if he'd been thrown against a wall. The piercing sound paralyzed him while every visual image in his Box got snuffed out. Each pixel of color sputtered into darkness.

Corgan threw his arms over his ears to try to block the excruciating pain, but the sound kept blasting. "No!" he wailed, curling up in a ball. "Stop!" Nothing helped. The screeching shrilled louder and louder, stabbing his brain. His body shook in spasms. Then he thrashed with convulsions, his arms and legs lurching out at angles unnatural to human anatomy.

Suddenly it was over.

He lay helpless, unable to move, tears streaming from his eyes, blood from his nose, and moans from his lips.

"Get up. You're not hurt," Mendor the Father told him. "I never thought it would be necessary to use that kind of punishment on you, Corgan. But you were out of control."

He must have lost track of time. Had he lost consciousness? Because now it was Mendor the Mother leaning over him, and Mendor had never been able to morph that quickly from Father to Mother. "Wipe your nose, dear boy. The bleeding's already stopped. Here, take a sip of water," she was telling him, but even before he could swallow, Mendor the Father loomed over him again.

Corgan squeezed his eyes tightly and then opened them, bewildered. "These are the rules!" Mendor the Father was saying harshly. "You will be given an hour to pull yourself together, to prepare for today's practice. From now on, at practice, you will not speak without permission, unless you need to communicate with the other two members of your team about the practice session. Nothing else! You will focus all your attention on one objective: winning the War. Is that clear?"

Corgan nodded. Just that small movement made his head pound. Instantly Mendor the Mother was there, rubbing his forehead.

"From this moment forward," Mendor the Father thundered, "you will obey all orders. You will always tell the truth. When the time comes, you will wage the War with honor. You must promise this."

"I promise," he whispered.

"You give your word? Good. I trust you."

"We'll warm up slowly." Mendor was doing the instructing, but Corgan sensed that members of the Supreme Council had been summoned and hovered close by, watching Corgan. Sharla and Brig had not yet appeared.

Though he was still hoarse, Corgan had recovered from the high-decibel shock waves. He no longer felt frightened because he knew exactly what he was supposed to do: follow orders, tell the truth, and win the War honorably.

"Recite the pledge," Mendor ordered.

Corgan raised his hand, which still trembled

very slightly. "I promise to wage the War with courage, dedication, and honor."

This time he took definite notice of the word "honor"—it slammed his brain with such an impact, he winced.

"Begin."

The figures of a common board game appeared, three-dimensionally, in front of him.

Chess! Corgan almost smiled. They'd given him *chess*, an easy game like that. To make amends for his punishment? But when he began to play, the chess pieces turned monstrous. The most horrible images They could throw at him materialized on the chess board, and grew enormous until they towered over him: An octopus slithered over the board and reached for Corgan's hands with slimy, sucking tentacles; huge, mossy-scaled, misshapen fish gaped toward him with undulating mouths. . . .

"Confront your fears, Corgan," Mendor urged him.

"What, these? I'm not afraid of these." Allotting no more than seven-tenths of a second to each chess piece, Corgan demolished them, one by one.

"Play again!" he ordered. "Where's Brig? I'd like some strategy input from Brig, please. He needs the practice."

"I'm here, Corgan." Brig's image appeared, as ordinary as always, but his eyes looked haunted. "I'll try to provide useful input," he said softly.

"See that you do." Corgan couldn't stand to look at Brig when he said that. Couldn't think about Brig's eyes or about Brig in Reprimand or anything except the practice game. Had to focus all attention on one objective. Play to win.

Swiftly, the two of them dispatched the chessmen to monster hell. Then Sharla appeared, and the team moved on to harder games, playing for an hour without a break. The three of them performed well, their skills blending seamlessly.

"Splendid!" Mendor the Mother said. "Go to your Clean Rooms now. You'll meet again later for further practice."

The images of Sharla and Brig vanished instantly, and Mendor said, "Why are you waiting, Corgan? Off to the Clean Room with you, like a good boy, and when you come back, you can choose a nice scene of galaxies to go with your dinner. Stars and planets and comets—"

"No, thank you." He'd already seen real stars. Virtual galaxies could mean nothing to him from now on. "I'd like the Isles of Hiva again, please," he said. First, though, he had to deal with a nagging puzzle. "Mendor, I timed you once. It takes you fourteen and thirty-three hundredths seconds to morph from Mother to Father. Or from Father to Mother. Has that changed? Has it speeded up?"

"What a strange question, Corgan. No, it hasn't. Why did you ask that?"

"Never mind." Biting his lip, Corgan moved into the tunnel.

When he returned from the Clean Room, his steak was waiting. Not soybeans in disguise—this was real beef, hot and perfect. So he'd been forgiven completely, and his trespasses were to be forgotten. Be a good boy, do what you're ordered, always tell the truth, and you'll get steak. Were Sharla and Brig getting real meat, too?

A faint drumbeat throbbed as the Isles of Hiva surrounded him, the ocean waves rushing toward him, flecked with foam, while sea birds cruised on air currents above his head. But he couldn't really enjoy it. He was too puzzled about why Mendor had seemed to morph so fast.

He considered the possibilities. Maybe he'd been partly unconscious. He knew that a condition known as unconsciousness existed, where a person's brain shut down for a certain period of time, although he'd never personally experienced such a thing.

The other possibility was more ominous. What if the sound-shock punishment had damaged his time-splitting ability? But why would Mendor or the Council take a chance of hurting him when the War was so close?

"Mendor," he asked the Mother Figure, "has anyone else with my kind of time skill ever been sound-shocked before?"

"Why talk about unpleasant things?" Mendor

replied. "The incident is over. Finished. It's best forgotten now."

"Please, I need you to answer that."

"All right. If you promise to eat while I talk," Mendor fussed. "Sound-shock is used as punishment because it's effective and causes no permanent damage. Admittedly it's unpleasant while it lasts—"

"It's a lot more than unpleasant!"

"—but it has been fully documented in hundreds of cases and it's totally harmless. Eat, now. Your steak must be getting cold."

The steak tasted flat but he chewed and swallowed to satisfy Mendor. "You didn't tell me what I asked you, though. Has anyone with my time-splitting power been sound-shocked before?"

"Corgan . . ." Mendor the Mother's warm image wrapped around him. "Don't you understand? There *is* no one else who can calculate time like you do. There never has been. You're unique. You're a mutation, with a skill never before known to humankind."

"I'm a *Mutant*?"

"No, a mutation, in the best possible sense of the word. That's how the human race evolved, you know. How *everything* evolved. The superior mutations, the exceptional ones, have always thrived and flourished; the weak ones die out. Now finish that last bite, and then, would you like to take a nice little stroll across the beach before it's time to practice again? You'll have an extra practice session this evening to make up for the time lost this morning."

"No. No walk." It was too much for him to handle. He felt overwhelmed by all that had happened that day, by all that had been done to him, and now, by what Mendor had just told him. Shoving it out of his mind, he said, "I think we should get back to practice right away."

Mendor beamed. "What a dedicated, industrious boy!"

He was neither of those things. He had an urgent need to check his timing, to make sure it was functioning right, and to see Sharla, to try to contact her with his eyes. Had she understood what he tried to tell her before the blast of sound knocked him senseless?

But for the first hour, he practiced alone: Precision and Sensitivity training again. Lately They'd been doubling—even tripling—his P and S sessions. Using electromagnetic energy to move a twelve-centimeter-square patch of laser light seemed an odd exercise to concentrate on, but Corgan asked no questions.

Later, when the team assembled for practice again, Sharla, Brig, and Corgan glanced furtively at one another. After that Sharla avoided Corgan's eyes. When they recited the pledge this time, she seemed to be saying the same words he did.

They played hard, doing Triple Multiplex, and Corgan was relieved to realize that his timing ability worked fine. But as he checked the score, he saw that it was a little lower than usual. "Mendor, is that score right? Oh, sorry, Mendor, I should have asked permission before I spoke."

"Forgiven. I will double-check the score, but you must rest now. Tomorrow will be another day for practice."

As Corgan settled into the aerogel, time ticked away in discrete hundredth-second intervals inside his head. Perfectly. Yet, during that incident earlier in the day—whether it had been brief or otherwise, he didn't know—he hadn't been able to calibrate time. And his score tonight had been a little off. *If* it was true that he was having a bit of trouble with his timing, why should it affect his playing ability? Calculating time was one kind of skill and playing games with his hands was another entirely different skill, and the first shouldn't have an impact on the second.

At eleven o'clock he stood up and moved toward the door, knowing it was futile to bother, but doing it just the same.

He couldn't find the opening. In the dark, he felt all over for a way out, but the exit was gone. He was locked in.

What had he expected? That They'd let those secret meetings in the tunnel keep happening, now that They knew?

He'd ruined everything when he confessed. Now he'd never see the real Sharla again. Never be able to touch her. That, on top of everything else that had come crashing down on him today, crushed him with despair.

He slammed his fists into the soft aerogel.

Eight

The next day Sharla wouldn't meet his eyes, and Brig wouldn't *stop* looking at him. Spooky little Brig, pleading without words. Because no matter how hard Corgan tried, he couldn't match his usual high score in the War-game practice.

He was only a little off, and no one said anything, but everyone noticed.

That night the door was locked again. In his sleep, Corgan ground his teeth and pounded his aerogel pillow.

The following morning he got up and ran a thousand meters on the virtual racing track in his Box, then lifted weights until his biceps burned. When he took his place at practice, Mendor stated, "Ten days remain until the War. According to the rules agreed upon by the three confederations, this is the day your team will be introduced to the actual format the War will take."

Corgan tensed as the Box filled with surround-images of hills and dusty ground, pockmarked by shallow depressions. A shell exploded right next to him, sending up a plume of orange flame and smoke and a shower of dirt that fell back on his head. He grabbed his ears—since his high-decibel punishment, he shuddered at every loud noise.

"That's the way wars were fought seventy years ago," Mendor explained. "Fortunately for you, the War you're going to fight won't be quite as brutal, but it will have all the noise of the old-fashioned wars."

Corgan frowned. That didn't sound good.

"You will not see the other two teams," Mendor went on. "We know nothing about them except that each team consists of three players. Age, gender, area of expertise—none of that is known." Mendor's harsh voice softened a little. "Conversely, they know nothing about the three of you, either.

"Now, here are the rules: The images you play with will be of actual soldiers in battle dress. All the moves were programmed to recreate real warfare as it was fought at the beginning of the twenty-first century. Tanks, fighter aircraft, aerial bombardment, and artillery—they'll all be directed against you. Not to mention poison gas attacks, toxic agents, chemical and bacterial contaminants. *Your only defense will be to evade these assaults. You will never go on the offensive. All you are allowed to do is protect your troops by moving them to safe ground.*"

Corgan asked, "May I speak, Mendor? If we

can't attack, if all we can do is stay out of the way, how do we win the War?"

"Patience!" Mendor the Stern Father demanded. "I'll explain the rest of the rules later. For now I want you, Corgan, to move the soldiers around to get used to the feel of them. Brig will observe."

It was as though they were real people, perfectly three-dimensional, with distinct facial features and skin colors, but each one was no bigger than Corgan's hand. They milled around aimlessly over the pockmarked ground.

"Pull them together, Corgan. Line them up in platoons," Brig instructed over the audible connector.

Corgan reached out too quickly and obliterated a dozen troops. Brig gasped. Stricken, Corgan looked up at Mendor.

As though trying not to reproach Corgan in front of everyone, Mendor spoke quietly. "Isn't it obvious, Corgan, that all your Precision and Sensitivity training has been for this one purpose? You must move your soldiers the way you moved the laser square: by compressing electromagnetic force. Never touch them directly! They have been designed so that your hand will set them in motion when you come to within five hundred microns of each image."

Sharla spoke then. "I could change the codes to increase the magnetic force field a little," she suggested. "That way Corgan could move the images from farther away—like, seven hundred microns?"

"No!" Mendor was adamant. "The War rules won't allow that. Corgan can do this. It's what he's been trained for. Try again, Corgan."

Concentrating so hard that sweat broke out on his forehead, Corgan moved his hands toward the images. Although the soldiers looked real and solid, they were only millions of holographic projections of colored lasers, as delicate as moonbeams. If he pushed just a fraction too hard, his hand went through them and they died.

Now he understood why Mendor and the Council had always fussed so much about his hands. Why he'd had to practice countless hours reaching to within a hair's breadth of the laser square. Strength, stamina, speed—all of them mattered, but not as much as P and S. In this War, Precision and Sensitivity would be the winning factor.

By the middle of the morning, Corgan had gotten the hang of it, sort of. "Now," Mendor said, "the object of all this is to move your soldiers onto designated territory: the top of that hill, where the flag is. Of course the other two teams will be trying to do the same: to get their soldiers onto the same hill. The team to reach the hill with the largest number of surviving troops will be declared the winner. It's as simple as that."

"That's it?" Corgan asked.

"That's it. Your job is to move the soldiers without touching them, using electromagnetic force. Sharla's job is to change the trajectory codes of artillery launched against our troops. At the same time she must jam the codes the other teams use as they try to block barrages aimed at their own troops. It won't be easy—destruction will rain so thick and fast on all three teams that most of it will be impossible to stop."

"I'll do my best," Sharla said.

"All the bombardment, against all three teams, will originate at the same source," Mendor continued, "the Coordinated Confederations Command Control Center."

"Wait a minute! I mean, do I have your permission to speak, Mendor? Are you saying that the three confederations are banding together to blast their own armies?" Corgan asked. "That's a weird way to fight a war."

"It will be perfectly fair. Each explosion, each assault, each demolition will be counted out equally. Each team gets the same amount of bombardment, down to the last bullet. War-game designers from all three confederations have worked for years to make this War scrupulously equitable."

Corgan didn't know what "scrupulously equitable" meant, but he figured it must be the same as "fair."

"It will be a war of defense," Mendor told them. "Strictly defense. The team with the largest number of surviving troops on the hill at exactly five P.M.—wins!"

"What about Brig?" Corgan asked. "What's his job?"

"Brig will be the only member of your team who witnesses the entire, overall War scene. At every moment, he will know how many soldiers remain in each of the three armies. He will see where they all are in relation to the hill. He will communicate this information to both you, Corgan, and to Sharla, and he will tell you where and when to move your soldiers. And while your team is busy communicating and changing codes and dispatching troops . . ." Mendor paused for a long moment. ". . . Bombs, mines, and heat-seeking missiles will be exploding; machine guns will fire on your soldiers; poison gas, chemical weapons, and all the other destruction that we talked about will be deployed against you."

Corgan leaned back and let the breath he'd been holding rush out between his lips.

It had been a hard day. Corgan felt drained. Learning to manipulate the virtual soldiers, to protect them from twenty deadly explosions all hitting them at the same time—in spite of Sharla's skill at deflecting shells and air missiles, there were land mines and ground fire—it was tough work! The only thing that gave him hope was that it must have been just as hard for the other two teams that would play in the War. It was the first day of real practice for them, too.

Still! Corgan hadn't played well. The harder he tried, the more mistakes he made. He'd concentrated as hard as he could, and tried to focus himself completely on the job he had to do, but it wasn't turning out right. He kept snuffing out his own troops.

"There are so many of them!" he'd protested to Mendor. "In P and S training I only had to move one laser square at a time."

"In P and S training your hand needed to come within two hundred microns of the laser square. Here, the distance is greater—five hundred microns. That makes it easier. You should have little trouble maneuvering more figures at once. Concentrate!"

He'd concentrated until his brain went numb. The day dragged out so long he couldn't wait for practice to end.

That night, wearily, he got up at eleven o'clock and moved to check the door, not expecting it to be open. But it was. He went through it, to find Sharla and Brig waiting for him in the tunnel. Without a word, he threw his arms around both of them. They sank together onto the cold floor, arms entwined, and just kept hugging each other.

"They locked me in," Corgan whispered. "Were you locked in, too? Last night and the night before?"

"Yes. They changed the codes."

"Couldn't you break them?"

"I didn't try too hard," Sharla answered, "because there was a lot to think about."

"So why did They let us out now?"

Neither Sharla nor Brig answered right away, and Corgan's mind jumped to something more important. "Sharla, could you understand what I was trying to tell you the other day, before They hit me with the sound shock?"

"I got it. When They had you in Reprimand, you told Them about our meetings," Sharla answered.

"I—I'm sorry." Corgan dropped his head into his hands. "I feel so bad!"

Brig chimed in, "So Corgan the Bold and Magnificent cracked under pressure, while Brig the Weak and Ugly held out. Maybe big and strong isn't the same as brave."

"Stop it, Brig," Sharla told him. "It didn't really make any difference. They would have known, anyway, as soon as They read the morning reports. Or maybe They already knew, before They even put Corgan into Reprimand."

"What?" Corgan raised his head. "What morning reports?"

"Our chemical analysis reports. They must have been all out of balance. . . ."

"He doesn't know what you're talking about," Brig said, tapping Corgan on the head. "Corgan the Squealer is also Corgan the Clueless."

Corgan knocked Brig's arm away. "You'd better

explain things," he said to Sharla. "What chemical analysis?"

She moved a little apart from him. "Don't you ever wonder about it," she began, "that everything from your body is collected? Your sweat gets sucked up in the vapor tube when you're sanitized. Your body fluids and solids go into the flush tube. Even the breath you exhale gets collected in the aerogel. Didn't you ever try to guess why?"

Corgan shook his head, then remembered they couldn't see him in the dark. "No."

"Everything your body puts out gets analyzed, Corgan. Every day. They want to make sure all your physical systems are working right. You've missed a lot of sleep lately—that shows up in the reports. And your midnight run the other night: Think what that did to your endorphin count."

"And me," Brig said. "I was so scared that night my adrenaline went off the charts. Sharla told me. She broke those codes and read our charts."

"The Council's not stupid," Sharla went on, "and we left enough clues for Them to figure it out. Brig's torn suit, the smashed dome on the hover car . . ."

After the first astonishment, rage began to seep in. "So They knew all along! And They took me on that guilt trip into Reprimand all for nothing. They must have been laughing Their stupid heads off back there behind Their invisible barriers."

"I don't think so." Sharla gripped Corgan's

shoulder to calm him. "Really, all They want is for us to win this War."

Shaking off her hand, Corgan exploded with fury. "They talk about truth and honor, and then They do that to me! Play me like a puppet! Blast my brain with sound shocks! All for their dumb bloody War. That's all They care about. Not us! They only care about Their War. So we win the War for Them, and what do we get out of it?"

"Real steak?" Brig suggested.

"I can't believe what you just told me about Them analyzing my sweat and my . . . it's *my* body, isn't it? They don't own it."

"They created it, Corgan," Sharla said quietly. "Yours and mine and Brig's and quite a few hundred others that didn't turn out so well. They manufactured us, so I guess They think we belong to Them."

"Damn Them!" Corgan cried, using the only strong word he knew. "So I'm supposed to give Them everything They ask for. And what do They give me?"

"They're giving you us," Sharla answered. "Brig and me."

"Think about it," Brig said. "They know all about what's been going on between us, and still They let us out of our Boxes tonight. To be together. Aren't you wondering why?"

If he'd wondered about it a little earlier, it had been driven out of his mind by bitterness over what he'd just learned. "So you must know the answer to that question, Big-Brain Strategist, or you wouldn't be asking me," Corgan said. "Are you going to impress me, or do I guess?"

"Just think about it," Brig said again.

With great effort, Corgan pushed back his anger so he could speculate. Why was he let out tonight, after being locked in his Box the previous two nights? What was different about tonight? What was different about today? Yesterday? Then it came clear.

"My scores," he said. "They were lower. Did the Council think I was holding back?"

"Possibly," Brig answered.

"No, I don't think so," Sharla told them. "It was pretty clear you were doing the best you could. But your edge was gone. I think They decided to give you what you wanted—meaning meeting us in the tunnel—to see if your playing will improve."

Fear knotted Corgan's stomach. "What if it doesn't? I really was trying. Honest!"

"I believe you," Sharla said.

Brig declared, "They keep trying to manipulate us like we do the virtual soldiers. What we need is a plan of our own. And I happen to have one. I'm a Strategist, remember? And it's a great plan." He wiggled himself comfortably between the two of them, picked up their arms and wrapped them around him as if he were a doll.

"So what's the plan?" Corgan demanded. "Not that I'm going to need it or anything. I just had a minor performance lapse. It happens to lots of people. By tomorrow I'll be playing better than ever."

"Well, just in case you mess up again, we need a fall-back plan," Brig said, "and I really look forward to sharing my brilliance with you both. But not till you pay me what you owe me."

"What are you talking about?" Corgan tried to push him away, but Brig clung tightly to Corgan's arm.

"Remember where we were supposed to go the other night?" Brig asked.

"The Mutant Pen."

"Well, we never got there, did we? And I want to go. So after the two of you take me there tomorrow night, I'll tell you my plan." He giggled. "And I guarantee it'll knock you over with its sagacity."

Sagacity! What a toad! This time Corgan managed to shove Brig away, using more force than necessary. "We won't need any brilliant plan," he growled. "I'll be great tomorrow. Anyway, what makes you think They'll let us meet again tomorrow night?"

"Just wait and see," Brig said.

Nine

The next morning at practice, Sharla held up both hands and wiggled her fingers and thumbs. "Exercising," she announced for the benefit of Them, wherever They were. Corgan knew what she really meant. Ten o'clock. The three of them could meet in the tunnel at ten that night rather than at eleven. Now that everyone knew what was going on and the policy was to keep silent about it, why wait that extra hour?

At ten he didn't even grope for the door of his Box; he walked right through it. Was it his imagination or did the tunnel seem slightly brighter? Sharla and Brig were waiting even farther along the corridor than before, because, Sharla explained when he reached them, she wanted to save Brig from walking more than he had to.

"So just carry me, then," Brig said to Sharla, lifting his arms.

Corgan didn't understand why Sharla found this so amusing. "Forget it. Let me carry the little monkey," he said, and swung Brig up onto his shoulders.

Pummeling Corgan with his small, crooked feet, Brig squealed, "I want Sharla! Give me to Sharla!"

Corgan grabbed the flailing little feet and held them so tightly that Brig couldn't move. "Keep quiet, or I'll bounce you on the floor," he threatened. "Or maybe I'll just bounce you." Corgan broke into a trot, loosening his grip on Brig so the stunted boy whipped around on Corgan's back, his big head wobbling from side to side on his spindly neck.

"Stop it, Corgan. You'll hurt him," Sharla pleaded, but Brig only whacked Corgan on the side of the head.

"*Me* hurt *him*! He's the one pounding my ears!" Corgan grabbed Brig by one ankle, held him upside down at arm's length, and started shaking him up and down.

"Corgan, *stop it*! Look at him—he's almost convulsing!"

He was. With laughter. Giggling so hard he could barely talk, Brig gasped, "Ole Ape Arms thinks I'm a co-co-co-co-co-nut. He's sh-sh-shaking me out of a tree."

"You two are disgusting," Sharla scoffed. "I hope They're watching you. It's scary that the fate of the Western Hemisphere depends on you two idiots."

"*I'm* not an idiot," Brig yelled. "*Corgan's* the idiot. He didn't play any better at practice today, just like I said he wouldn't!"

Corgan fought the urge to drop Brig on his head. Instead he set him down feet first, so hard that Brig's legs buckled. In a beat, the little Mutant jumped back up and cried, "But the Federation doesn't need to worry about Corgan being such a pathetic flop—"

"Flop! You little—," Corgan sputtered.

"—'cause *you'll* save us, Sharla. You'll carry us to victory. And you can start by carrying *me!* Right *now!*"

"—you little slug! I'm gonna drag you back to your Box right now and you can forget all about going to the Mutant Pen—"

In the almost dark corridor, Sharla grabbed Corgan's arm. "Get control! Don't let him make you so mad. Just because he's acting like a baby—"

"Yeah. A baby monster. A baby fascist dictator. A baby leech, a baby pervert—"

"Oh, Corgan! Show a little sensitivity! Don't you ever think about what it would be like to be *him*?" She broke away, went back to Brig, and picked him up. "We're not too far from the hover cars, Brig," she said as he put a strangle hold around her neck. Corgan couldn't see too well in the dark, but he imagined Brig smirking at him.

He wanted to punch the walls in anger but he couldn't take a chance on hurting his hands. Flop!

111

That was what Brig had called him. He searched his vocabulary for all the nasty names he could think of to spit back at Brig, but Corgan's list of expletives was pretty limited. Instead, he fired off a couple of swift kicks at the empty air, and by the time they reached the hover-car track, he had himself under control. Why let Brig spoil his time with Sharla? Ignore the brat, he told himself. Hard as it is, ignore him.

At that minute Jobe materialized out of the shadows. "Hi, Sharla," he said, waving a wrench in greeting. "Looking for a ride?"

"Yeah, Jobe. You looking for a tip?"

"Not tonight," Jobe answered. "Don't need nothin' tonight. You and your buddies just go right ahead and get in the hover car. I stopped it for you so you can climb in easy. It's been polished and disinfected nice and clean."

Inside, after Jobe closed the dome, Sharla said, "No running beside the track and trying to dive into a moving car this time."

"I want to go straight to the Mutant Pen," Brig announced. "I hope the cars don't jam up again."

"I have a feeling everything's going to go as smooth as soy sauce tonight," Sharla told him.

Corgan leaned back into the molded seat, getting pleasure from looking at Sharla in the light. "Your cheeks are flushed," he said. "They're like— like the sun when it first comes up and it brushes the bottom of the clouds over the ocean." Corgan wasn't good at pretty speeches; he must sound like a dolt.

Sharla seemed to like it, though. She smiled and said, "I wish I knew how clouds look when a real sun rises over a real ocean."

Brig bounced in the seat between them and grinned, showing his small, crooked teeth.

"What's into you, Strategist?" Corgan asked him.

"Nothing." Tilting back his big head on his thin neck, Brig looked through narrowed eyelids first at Corgan, and then at Sharla, all the while grinning at them like a clown.

"Who knows what he's up to," Sharla said, shrugging. "But here we are. At the Mutant Pen."

It was as if everything had been prepared for them. The hover car stopped and the bubble dome opened at a touch. When they got out, they found themselves next to a wall that was already transparent; Sharla didn't need to work her code box. A little stool, just the right size for Brig to climb on, stood near the clear section of the wall.

Silent, the three of them stared through the opening.

Inside were babies, mostly—or at least undersized, stunted, helpless little creatures that looked more or less like human babies, lying in cribs. The ones who had arms waved them; some had grasping, prehensile, clawlike fingers that could hold little rattles and dolls. Only a few of the thirty or more Mutants in the Pen looked older than two. Only a few had the right number of eyes, ears, fingers, arms, and legs.

Her voice shaking, Sharla said, "I didn't think there were still so many genetic failures."

Brig had his face pressed against the wall. "I know him," he said, pointing to a big Mutant who sat in a corner, rocking on the floor, his arms crossed over his bloated chest. "That's Rojean. He was there when I was there."

Rojean had no legs. He swayed back and forth, eyes dull, face expressionless.

"Rojean's not dumb," Brig said. "When I was in the Pen, he could talk. Why's he just sitting there like that?"

Some of the older children rolled or crawled on the floor, if they had enough limbs to propel themselves. Corgan wanted to close his eyes to blot it all out, but at the same time he felt compelled to watch. The scene horrified him, yet overwhelmed him with pity. Brig had said that most of them died young. Maybe that was for the best, and yet Brig—what if Brig hadn't lived? Brig was brilliant. He was irritating to the infinite power, but he was smart enough to have been pulled out of that awful Pen, and to take part in a War for the most valuable commodity on Earth: uncontaminated land. In spite of his deformities, Brig was a useful human being. What did it matter if he looked like—those things in there?

The Mutants. Brig was a Mutant. And Corgan was a mutation, Mendor had said. It seemed the only difference between a mutation and a Mutant was that one turned out right and one turned out wrong. *I could have been one of them,* Corgan thought, staring into the Pen.

I could have been Brig.

Imagine what it would be like to be him, Sharla had said. Corgan tried to imagine. *Undersized. Weak. Ugly. And knowing every minute that people found him repulsive.*

Tentatively, he put his hand on top of Brig's head and ruffled the flame-colored hair. Brig turned his huge, sorrowful eyes to Corgan. "When I was in Reprimand," he said as tears streamed down his cheeks, "They told me how kind They'd been to take me out of the Pen. They said how lucky I was to be alive, because from now on, Mutants like me won't be allowed to live."

"What!" Corgan couldn't believe he'd heard it right.

"They said resources are too limited now and Mutants take up too much time and effort and they don't pay anything back. From now on, when they're gestating in the laboratory and tests show that they won't be normal, they'll be destroyed. And maybe even these ones in here . . ." He pointed through the window. "The Supreme Council's trying to decide whether to let them keep on living."

"Keep on? . . . That can't be true," Corgan muttered.

"It's true, all right. And They kept saying how kind They were to me because not only was I allowed to live, but They've given me an important job and They've cared for me and . . ." Brig leaned his big head on Corgan's chest and sobbed.

"Come on, don't do that," Corgan said, lifting him up. "Let's get out of here, Sharla. This was a bad idea."

The hover car stood waiting, its dome still open. "It'll be a long ride back," Sharla said when they were inside. "The track loops through this whole city. It'll be nice, though; we can lean back and look up at the stars."

Brig lay between them with his head still on Corgan's chest, his small hands crossed underneath his chin. The anger Corgan had felt earlier was now gone. Trying to choose his words carefully so he wouldn't hurt Brig any further, Corgan said, "Genetic engineering might not be such a great idea—for any of us. I mean, why does it have such a high failure rate?"

"Do you know how many genes are in a human being's DNA?" Sharla asked him. "Two hundred thousand. Each human cell has about forty meters' worth of DNA that's only a couple of angstroms wide. And the scientists have to locate the one little part of that DNA that holds the trait they want, and chop it out, and splice it into another section of

DNA. And they don't even have any decent equipment here. All the good stuff, like automated DNA sequencers, is still out there in the contaminated world where we can't get it. No wonder we have failures."

Sharla looked down; Brig had fallen asleep on Corgan's lap. "Poor little guy. He's not very strong," she whispered, stroking his damp red hair. "It's kind of a miracle that he's made it this far. Most times, after the gene splicing, the altered cells die, or just don't grow, or else they're so obviously weird that they get destroyed right in the beginning."

"How do you know so much about it?" Corgan asked.

"Because," she said, "that's what I want to do with my life. I want to be a genetic engineer. I was bred to work with codes. Cryptanalysis or DNA analysis—it's all coding."

He wasn't especially surprised. Mostly he felt curious about just how she'd been bred, and what had made her the way she was. But he didn't want to pry. Anyway, he was even more curious about himself.

"Where did I come from?" he asked. "I mean, how did they make me? Do you know?"

"Sure. I looked you up. You got your fast reflexes and precise hand control from your mother and father."

"You mean Mendor?"

"Corgan, Mendor is a *program*. You're a human being. I mean your biological parents. The sperm and the egg that were taken out of the frozen-tissue bank and combined in a test tube to make you. That, plus some traits spliced in from donor tissue."

"Does that mean? . . ." He was trying hard to understand it. "That I have two parents, or more than that? And anyway, who are they? Or who were they?"

Sharla answered, "It says in your records that half of your original genetic material came from— get ready for this—a champion tennis player who died in 2057."

"Mother or father?" He could say those words without any emotional tug, because there were no human memories attached to them.

"Mother, if you want to use the old-fashioned term. The other half, the father half I guess you'd call it, was a surgeon famous for reattaching severed nerves. Little tiny nerve endings." She smiled at him. "Then you got bits of DNA from other people added to you for time measurement, stamina, and hand strength."

Corgan raised his agile right hand and flexed it. He flexed his biceps, stretched his arm across the back of the seat, and reached to pull Sharla against him so their cheeks rested together. When she turned to face him, he kissed her. He put both arms around her and kissed her again.

"Stop," she whispered.

"Why? Because of Brig? He's asleep."

"No. Because I asked you to stop."

Corgan leaned back, confused. "That time before," he said, "you let me then. In fact, you were the one who kissed me first."

"It's different now," she said.

"How is it different?"

She turned away from him and looked out the dome of the hover car, although there was nothing much to see in the dark corridor. "Because I hardly knew you then, and now I really like you."

"*What?*" It made no sense to him.

"Before, I was just sort of—I'm sorry—playing with you, Corgan. It wasn't fair. You're so innocent."

Hurt, he pulled his arm away. "You make it sound like a disease—being innocent," he told her, sulking.

"It's not your fault," she said. "They've kept you away from everyone else. They've filled you full of Their thoughts and Their words and you only think what They want you to think and say what They tell you to say—"

Is that so wrong, he wondered. Every time he tried to do or say something outside the rules he got yelled at or punished. He couldn't be like Sharla, who did and said anything she pleased and always came out of it just fine.

"Sharla," he asked, "when we recite the pledge, are you saying something different?"

119

She smiled. "So you noticed. I just make up some nonsense words that sound pretty much the same."

"Like what?"

"You say it first, Corgan. Repeat the pledge."

He almost raised his hand but caught himself in time; if he had, she'd probably have laughed and counted it as one more sign of his innocence. "I pledge to wage the War with courage, dedication, and honor," he said slowly, seriously considering the meaning for the first time in a long while.

"Okay, here's a couple of my variations." Sharla did raise her hand and, in a mocking, singsong voice, recited, "*I wedged the cage's door with birds and red carnations, Your Honor. Or, I educated Lori, urging meditation upon her. Or, I fled the raging boar with furry dead—*"

"You're making fun of the pledge," he accused her.

"Why not? The Council forces me to say it. They can't make me believe in it. To me, the War's just a silly game."

Frowning, perplexed, he studied her in the soft light. She was so clever and so pretty that she filled him with all kinds of longings, but she made him feel off balance. "Don't you believe in anything?" he asked her.

"Sure. I believe in myself."

Ten

"Brig, wake up. The ride's over. Time to go home." When Corgan lifted Brig, he felt dampness on his sleeve where Brig's sweaty head had lain against it for so long.

"Do you want to tell us your plan now before we get out of the hover car?" Sharla asked.

"No. Too tired. Tomorrow night." Brig wound his arms around Corgan's neck and went back to sleep.

"I'll carry him back to his Box," Corgan said. "Maybe we ought to meet earlier tomorrow night so he won't get so tired out."

"Okay. Nine o'clock tomorrow. 'Night, Corgan." She brushed his cheek with her lips, which was better than nothing, but not nearly as much as he would have liked.

After depositing Brig in his Box, Corgan walked slowly to his own. No sprinting tonight. It was past midnight. He was tired, too, and he needed to wake himself early in the morning to allow time for an intense physical workout. He flexed his hands, wondering what was wrong with him. In the last warm-up practice game of Triple Multiplex, his score had been off by a half percent. By itself that wasn't too significant, but added to his disappointing performance on the two previous days, he was down by a total of a percent and a half. That was significant, considering that his performance score should have been going *up* by that much margin each day, rather than down.

At six the next morning he rolled out of his aerogel bed, pulled on his running shorts, and did forty laps around the virtual track. After that he practiced with weights and after that he did fifteen minutes of finger-flexing exercises. Mendor the Mother watched all this but said nothing, except, "You'll have to sanitize yourself now to have time for breakfast. Your food intake is important, too, you know."

Later, when the team assembled in the Wargames room, Mendor the Stern Father announced, "We'll start without a warm-up practice this morning."

Corgan felt both relief and anxiety. Unless he practiced on games where his earlier scores were already recorded, he had nothing to measure his performance against. He wouldn't be able to tell whether he'd broken out of his slump and was starting to play better. On the other hand, at least he'd be spared from knowing it if he was playing worse. "May I speak, Mendor? Why is that?" he asked.

"Because in the actual Virtual War, which is *eight days from now*, there will be no warm-up. All three teams will begin the War at precisely nine A.M. and will play straight through till precisely five P.M. No breaks for meals, for Clean Rooms, not even to wipe the sweat from your brows. *Eight straight hours of war!*"

Corgan looked at Sharla, or at least at her virtual image, which was all he ever saw of her during these practices. First at Sharla, then at Brig. Both of them returned his stare with eyes that showed the same alarm he was feeling. No breaks at all during the War?

"Will we have a chance to practice nonstop like that before the War?" Corgan asked Mendor.

"No. That would be too much of a strain on your health. You must conserve your strength now to maintain your physical peak for the actual War. Which means all extracurricular activity should be limited from now on!" Mendor's eyes changed into narrowly focused red beams that bored into Corgan.

"Limited," Mendor had just said. Not "stopped." "Extracurricular activity" meant their meetings in the tunnel at night. They'd been given a little freedom, but since nothing was ever discussed in actual words, Corgan had to keep feeling his way through each situation and then trying to guess Mendor's meaning. He didn't like this; he was too tired to play doublespeak games.

It made him feel like he was slogging through glue. Why couldn't the Council and Mendor just say what They meant? He stretched his arms and yawned.

"Begin!" Mendor bellowed. Corgan scrambled into position, two seconds late.

If each coming day of practice was going to bring a new element to the War, Corgan hoped They'd added the worst one first. Because it was pretty bad. Blood! They'd thrown in very realistic-looking blood.

Before, when artillery had hit his soldiers, they'd fallen down in a clean simulated death. Today, heads got blown off, arms got severed, and blood spurted so far that Corgan involuntarily jerked back his hands to keep them from getting bathed in gore. And when he did that, he missed the chance to move his soldiers, so more of them got killed. He wanted to scream for Time-out, but for the past two days Time-out hadn't been allowed. He wanted to close his eyes; instead he forced himself to keep his attention on the game.

Brig seemed calm about the bloodshed. "Over there!" he'd shout into the audio connector. "Watch your flank, Corgan. *Move that platoon!* Pull them behind that wall."

Corgan felt his stomach heave as the simulated battleground grew sticky with blood. He swallowed hard and focused on his soldiers, forgetting that they were only virtual images no bigger than the height of his hand. He smelled ozone and smoke and chemicals—

"Gas attack!" Brig screamed. "Get them *out* of there, Corgan!"

It seemed to go on endlessly. When Mendor finally stopped the game, he glowered at Corgan. "That lasted a full minute longer than the prescribed two-hour interval for today," Mendor rebuked him. "Why didn't you call time? If this had been the real Virtual War, Corgan, you'd have forfeited the battle."

Mortified, Corgan dropped his head onto his folded arms.

It had happened again! He'd lost track of time! It wasn't that he'd been *unable* to count time; he'd just become so intent on what he was doing he'd *forgotten* to count time. At least that's what he told himself.

"Go to your Clean Rooms," Mendor ordered. "Then eat. If this were the real War, you'd still be fighting. No breaks. Remember that."

The afternoon practice was as brutal as the morning had been. When it was over, and after another bath, Corgan fell asleep over his dinner. He woke up, startled, with Mendor the Mother smoothing his hair and telling him to brush his teeth before bedtime.

He met Sharla and Brig in the tunnel that night at nine.

"Pick me up, Corgan," Brig whimpered. "I'm

too tired to stand. I didn't think it would be this hard."

Corgan lifted Brig and held him head-high to both himself and Sharla. "I wonder why They let us stay out so late last night," he said. "They knew what today would be like."

"I think They wanted to make a point," Sharla answered. "So we'd find out for ourselves that we can't keep losing sleep. From now on, we'll have to cut back to fifteen minutes again if we want to stay competitive. Because if you think today was bad, tomorrow will probably be worse."

The tunnel felt cold and was completely dark; Sharla had forgotten to bring the piezoelectric stone. The three of them huddled together for warmth. "You'd better tell us your plan quick, Brig," Corgan said. "They're trying to freeze us."

"Yeah, just to make sure we know They're still in charge," Brig agreed. "That's their strategy. My plan, okay . . . but I feel kind of bad, because I wanted to see your faces when I sprang it on you, and now I can't."

"Never mind," Sharla soothed him. "After we hear it, we'll tell you how we feel about it."

Brig shivered and his voice shook. "To begin with, They've conceded a few things to us, letting us make some choices, like how long we'll stay out here tonight. That shows how much They're depending on us. There are no back-up replacements for us, which means They need us *really* bad. So . . . if we demand a reward, They'll have to consider it."

"What reward? Come on, spit it out, Brig," Corgan urged.

"We win the War for Them, and They . . . for our reward . . ." He paused. Whether it was for dramatic effect or because Brig didn't feel too confident about what he was going to suggest, Corgan couldn't be sure.

"We make Them promise to let us live on the Isles of Hiva."

Corgan sucked in his breath. Sharla's arms tightened around both of them.

"Do you think They'd go for it?" Corgan asked.

"If you guys let me do the negotiating," Brig answered.

"You?" Corgan sputtered. Weird little Brig, to be trusted with something that enormous, that would change their lives?

Brig's voice still shook from the cold. "Sharla told me who my biological parents were," he said. "The male reproductive cell had been frozen for seventy-four years, which maybe is why I became a Mutant, 'cause that's probably way too long. Anyway, my natural father was the head coach for a basketball team called the Boston Celtics."

"What's basketball?" Corgan asked.

"It's a sport people played back in the old days.

It was fast paced and complicated and my biological father told all the players what to do. Perfect genetics to breed a Strategist. Plus, my mother was the head of a big law firm. She never lost a case in court." Brig giggled. "What a combination I am! I wish I could have met them."

"Then he got some extra DNA from a top-ranking diplomat," Sharla said. "I think Brig can negotiate."

"If you agree, I'm going to present our demand right before War games tomorrow morning," Brig said. "They probably won't give us an answer right away. But who knows? Maybe They will."

Corgan asked, "Do we have a chance?"

"Why not?" Sharla demanded. "We were bred for something like this, we've been trained for this particular job, and when it's over, They won't need us anymore. Will They even care where we go? I think it might work, Brig."

"Yeah, so do I," Brig agreed.

"That means," Corgan said, "from now on we have to play perfectly—no mistakes—to show we can win for Them."

Silence. Neither Brig nor Sharla said anything, and Corgan squirmed. Both of *them* had been playing just fine, all along.

"Look, I know my proficiency's been off," he said. "But I'm working on it. It's under control now."

After another pause, Brig mentioned, "You went a minute overtime today."

"I said I'm working on it!"

In the dark, he couldn't read their faces. "Hey, if They promise us the Isles of Hiva, I'll get my winning edge back for sure. I'll play my brains out."

"That's what we were hoping," Brig said. "I mean—"

"Anyway, we don't need to worry," Corgan said with bravado. "We're unbeatable. Even if we don't play as well as we used to, we're still way better than the other two teams. Mendor told me that."

"When?"

"What does it matter when? We were genetically engineered, remember? To be the best in the world. Right? Right, Sharla?"

Quietly, she answered, "So were the players on the other two teams."

"What!" both Corgan and Brig exclaimed in disbelief.

"All three teams will consist of genetically engineered players."

"How'd you find out?" Brig asked grimly.

"How do I find out *anything*?" she answered. "Trust me. It's true."

The coldness of the tunnel seemed to seep into Corgan's lungs, chilling his heart. Brig whimpered.

"Maybe I shouldn't have told you," Sharla said. "Anyway, like we talked about, we need to get more sleep. Let's not meet tomorrow night."

"Not meet? How are we going to communicate if there's something we need to say to each other?" Corgan asked, subdued.

"That's easy. I'm in touch with both of you over the audio connector," Brig answered. "I mean, Sharla tells me the code changes, and I tell Corgan the strategy changes. If Sharla wants to throw in a personal message, and if she keeps it real short, I can pass it on to you, Corgan."

"What about the other direction?" Corgan asked. "Can I send a message through you to Sharla?"

"Sorry. One-way is the best I can do. Sharla to Brig to Corgan."

"Okay. We're in this together. If we win the War, we go to the Isles of Hiva," Sharla said, taking both their hands. "It's a pact, right?"

In the dark, they squeezed each other's hands.

His voice choking up, Corgan said, "We have to win. Because more than anything else, I want to get out of this place. I want to feel real ocean waves and run on sand. And I want to be where things can be out in the open. No more sneaking around and being spied on every time we breathe. No more Them knowing everything and pretending not to. No more Them keeping back information like . . . like—"

"The truth about our competitors," Sharla finished.

Eleven

The next morning, before Brig had a chance to speak, Corgan announced, "Mendor, I request permission to discuss something."

He could see the alarm in Brig's eyes, that Corgan might say something to spoil his plan. Corgan shook his head to reassure him.

"Permission is granted," Mendor said. "Go ahead, Corgan."

"My team," Corgan began, "Sharla, Brig, and myself, need to see each other the way we really are. There's no reason any longer to show false images of Brig and Sharla. I know what they look like in real life."

He could almost hear Mendor's various programs whirring as he/she searched for instructions to handle this. Corgan was unmasking something that had been deliberately concealed.

Forty-six and thirty-one hundredths of a second passed while Mendor's image stayed dimmed. During that time Brig's and Sharla's virtual images were stopped in freeze-frame. Then, gradually, they faded in, changing right before Corgan's eyes. Into themselves.

"Thank you, Mendor," Corgan said.

Brig rose to his feet. Now he was only half as tall as he'd looked earlier. "I have a request, too," he said.

"You, too?" Mendor cried. "We're wasting time, but go ahead."

"I'll try to keep it brief," Brig answered, his voice frail, "but could you please ask the Council to come? They're the ones who will have to decide on my request. . . ."

This time only twenty seconds elapsed before Mendor said, "Go ahead. The Council is waiting."

"If . . . if you don't mind, I'd like to see Them, please," Brig said.

Immediately Their images became visible. They were seated in Their usual row of six, Their faces featureless as always. The Councillor with the echo-chamber voice said, "State your reason for this delay in the War-games practice."

"Yes, sirs. And . . . madames." Short, twisted, and homely, the true-to-life virtual image of Brig stood up to approach Them. He gave a funny little bow, bobbing his big head, and said, "The three of us on the War team respectfully wish to submit a proposal to your honors, the Supreme Council."

Six faceless, motionless images waited, saying nothing.

"We . . . uh . . . we want to discuss a reward," Brig said. "We want to negotiate."

"What reward do you want?" The words seemed to blare equally loudly from all six mouthless, faceless heads.

Brig's voice faltered a little. "We've practiced diligently. We will fight the War with total dedication and undivided loyalty."

Oh, Brig, get to the point, Corgan thought. Don't let Them spook you.

Brig stiffened, trying to make himself taller. "But after the War is over, whether we win or lose, You will have no further use for us. Is that correct?"

Silence. Then, "Losing is not acceptable."

Brig stammered, "You're absolutely right. We're not going to lose." He took a deep breath. "This is what we'd like to negotiate for. We want to go to the Isles of Hiva after the War. Corgan and Sharla and me. To live there."

Nothing moved. It was like an image-generator malfunction when the motion shut down. The seconds ticked off inside Corgan's brain—seventeen seconds and a fraction.

"We will take it under advisement," a frosty collective voice declared from the Council. "That's all. Now begin your practice."

Brig scurried back to his War-game position. So the big scene was over. Had it done any good at all? Corgan doubted it. Brig seemed to shrink into himself, looking even more deformed.

• • •

The next day was War Day Minus Six. It began with an explosion that shook Corgan to his toes, and Sharla was right. That day was worse than the day before, which had been worse than the day before that.

Added to the blood and gore were the soldiers' screams. Now when they died horribly with their eyes wide open in shock and terror, their cries twisted Corgan's insides.

"Focus! Focus!" Brig shouted. "Block out everything extraneous."

Corgan tried to ignore the screams and mutilation, tried to remind himself that these were only virtual images, not living people, but it was hard.

Yet, miraculously, when they broke for lunch, Mendor told Corgan that the Council had agreed to their request. If the team won the War, they'd be allowed to live on the Isles of Hiva. *If.* Corgan wanted to feel glad, to feel excited. A day earlier he would have. Now, knowing the kind of competition he was going to face in the War, he just felt scared.

When they met for the afternoon session, nothing more was said about the Isles of Hiva. No announcements—not a word, before or after they recited the pledge. Corgan wondered whether Sharla and Brig had been told, but he couldn't make eye contact with them. The game started then and it escalated in savagery until he felt physically sick.

He slept badly that night, his dreams filled

with horror. When he woke up whimpering, Mendor the Mother Figure was there to soothe him, stroking his forehead, speaking softly, humming the little lullabies she'd sung to him when he was young. "Think of Hiva," she crooned. "Win the War and the Isles are yours."

War Day Minus Five brought more land mines. He could hear Brig shouting, "Sharla, find the right code! Disable the mines. Corgan, move your troops to the rear. No, Corgan! You pushed too hard—you destroyed nine of them."

He kept having to choose: Move his troops to the left or to the right or straight ahead. There were never any clues which way they should go. If Corgan chose straight ahead the platoon might enter a minefield, where a dozen of them would get blown to pieces before he could move them out. Or the minefield might be to the left or to the right; planted at random, land mines were undetectable. Even worse than getting his troops blown up was penetrating them with his hands because he wasn't careful enough. That killed them just as dead as the land mines did.

He had the fastest reflexes ever recorded, but in this War, speed wasn't much help. It was precision that mattered. He could move his hands quickly to the images, but if he didn't stop in time to keep from touching them, he destroyed them. And when they died at Corgan's hands, they screamed horribly.

By midmorning, he found that he was hardening himself against the screams. That let him calculate better the microscopic distance between his hands and the troops, and not kill so many through his own clumsiness. All that fierce, unending slaughter was starting to lose its impact. Blood, torn limbs, disembowelment—it was all part of the game. Concentrate. Focus. Compress the force field. Feel it, he told himself. Don't notice the horror. When he stopped for lunch he could eat the food put in front of him, and not turn away, nauseated, as he'd done the day before.

"I think I might be toughening up," he mentioned to Mendor.

"Good for you," she answered.

His toughness lasted most of the afternoon, until a message came through Brig: "Sharla says no meeting tonight. Wait till tomorrow." That left a hollowness in him that he couldn't deal with then, couldn't even wonder about, because he had to fight. Had to concentrate. Had to move those troops without perforating them.

Even that night he couldn't mull over why she decided against meeting him, because he was so tired, the minute he fell into bed he fell asleep.

Then came War Day Minus Four, when They threw in the civilians. Women holding babies, old people who could barely walk, staggering along with their belongings, children fumbling onto the battlefield where land mines blew them apart. And beautiful girls, with haunting eyes, who held out their arms, beseeching him. He wanted to move the civilians to safety, but Mendor the Stern Father bellowed at him, "Forget those people! They are not your job. You are responsible only for your troops. Civilians mean nothing! Do you want to lose the War?"

And so he had to block out the images of the terrified girls. "They're not real, they're not real," he kept muttering to himself until his brain believed it even if his heart didn't.

"Message from Sharla," Brig managed to say. "Not tonight, either. Tomorrow, she promises."

Corgan cried in his sleep all night. "You must eat," Mendor the Mother coaxed him in the morning. "Look at this nice hot oatmeal."

"Made from soybeans," Corgan muttered.

"With brown sugar and milk . . ."

"Made from soybeans."

Mendor lost patience. "Corgan, you have to keep up your strength. You're not eating and you're not sleeping." She surrounded him so closely he felt as if she were smothering him. "Be a good boy now and eat your breakfast, or you won't be able to win the War. And if you don't win it, you'll lose the Isles of Hiva."

"Mendor, tell me the truth," he said. "Am I playing any better at all?"

Mendor dimmed. Then she said, "Be a good boy and eat your breakfast."

Hollow-eyed, he took his place on the morning of War Day Minus Three, steeling himself against compassion for the civilians, and against his need to see Sharla. He had one job to do: Move his troops to the designated area. Keep them alive as long as possible, because the rules of War stated that whichever side reached the goal first would win, but the number of troops left alive would also be factored in. If he got there first with hardly any soldiers left, he could still lose to the army that reached the goal a bit later, but with twice as many living soldiers.

That was the day the vicious air attacks began. Helicopters flew straight into his face. His instincts made him flinch, while Brig shouted in his loudest voice, "Ignore the air attack, Corgan. You lost three soldiers because your hand brushed them when you jerked away from that chopper." Very quietly, Brig added, "Sharla says tonight at nine."

When they met that night the tunnel was lighted, although only dimly. At least he could see her. "Where's Brig?" he asked.

"He didn't come. He needs all the sleep he can get. This is harder on him than it is on us." She put her arms around Corgan and they stood together, leaning against each other for comfort.

"Sharla, you're the only one I can ask. Tell me the truth. Am I playing any better?"

"No," she answered.

He slumped down onto the floor of the cold tunnel, arms crossed on his knees, head bent to lean on his arms. Sharla knelt beside him and, after a minute, said, "That doesn't mean we're going to lose the War; it only means you're not playing as well as you used to."

"So we're going to lose," he said. "No Isles of Hiva." His eyes stung with tears, and he turned away.

"Not necessarily." Lifting his face so he had to look at her, Sharla said, "I'm still tapping into the Council's daily records. What They're saying is that you're improving every day, but not fast enough. By now you should be able to move the troops without damaging any of them at all. But who knows? You still might be just as good as the other team leaders."

"I need to be better than they are, or we'll lose. What happened to me? I'm trying as hard as I can, but it won't come out right."

She didn't answer at first. Settling beside him, so that both of them were leaning against the cold steel wall, she reached for his hand. "Maybe I can help," she said.

"How? There's nothing wrong with the way you've been playing. You and Brig are great. It's me who's bombing out." He laughed bitterly. "Yeah, that's the right word for it. I bomb out every time I hear a bomb go off. The noise is making me crazy. And not just the explosions—the screams, and the—"

"Corgan, stop! Listen to me! I said I can help."

He turned to gaze at her, studying her face. If only he could win the War and spend the rest of his life on the sandy beaches of Hiva. If only he could forget the War and spend the rest of his life with Sharla.

"Don't say anything until you hear this, Corgan. The reason I waited till tonight to meet you was to see if—well, if when you got Hiva as an incentive—your playing would improve enough."

"And it didn't."

"I know. But remember the War rules They pounded into us over and over? 'If our team breaks a rule, even unintentionally, three times? . . .'"

"Right. We lose. And if we break a rule on purpose even once, we lose," Corgan said. "So what about it?"

"Remember me asking Mendor how the judges would know whether it was on purpose or not? It turns out the guidelines are pretty vague about how They figure out whether an infraction was really meant, or if it just happened by accident. So here's what I think."

She leaned close to him and spoke so softly in his ear that he could feel her breath on his cheek. "Right now, your hands have to come within five hundred microns of the soldiers to make them move. That's half a millimeter. But remember when I told Mendor I could enlarge the width of the force field to seven hundred microns?"

"And Mendor said it was against the rules."

"Right. But what if I mixed up one of my codes—accidentally, of course—and no one noticed for a while. It would be hard to prove it wasn't just a mistake. At seven hundred microns, you wouldn't have to be quite as careful. You could move your troops quicker without crushing as many."

His eyes widening, he drew back to stare at her. "What are you saying?"

"That you'd have easier control if the force field got compressed enough at seven hundred microns, instead of five hundred."

"You're talking about *cheating!*"

"I know it's risky, but it might give us enough of an edge to—"

"*Sharla! No!*" Corgan jumped to his feet.

"Don't say no so fast. The stakes are awfully high here—" Still on her knees, she held on to his hand, but he pulled it away. "Corgan, please, just think about it," she said, scrambling up to face him.

"I gave my word that I'd fight the War honorably," he told her.

"Yeah, well, you gave your word to obey, and to tell the truth, too, and here you are out in the tunnel with me, which we have been lots of times lately and Mendor and the Council are still pretending it isn't happening. So this whole phony

Supreme Council moralistic garbage is just one big lie anyway."

Backing away from her, he flattened himself against the cold wall. "That's Their problem. I can't control what They do, or how They run things. Only what I do."

"It's just—you don't know, I want so much to win—"

Corgan stared at her. "Once you told me the War was just a silly game. Now you're desperate to win it. What changed?"

"Nothing," she said. "I don't want to talk about it."

"Talk about what?"

"I said it's nothing. Just forget we had this whole conversation, okay?" She turned and would have walked away, but he grabbed her by the shoulders and swung her around.

"Sharla, I don't want you to cheat. I know you can probably pull off that code change and I wouldn't be able to stop you, but promise me you won't do it."

"Why should I? I *need* to win. And I don't care one bit about honor. Look around you, Corgan. Everyone cheats, everyone lies."

"I don't," he said. "Yeah, I've gone along with the pretending, but since that day after Reprimand, I've never spoken any lies and I've never disobeyed an order. I told Them I'd fight honorably. I'm going to."

She slammed her fists against his chest. "Why . . . *why* . . . is honor so important? It's just a word."

"No it isn't. It's a promise I make every day. Over and over. When I say the pledge."

"Can't you just leave it to me?" she begged. "You don't even have to know it's happening. You *won't* know. Those codes are easy! I can change them and *no one* will know!"

"That's not good enough," he said. "I need to trust you."

Suddenly she collapsed against him and began to cry. "All right! You're so damn noble! I'll give you what you want. I don't believe in the system or the Council or the Federation or anyone in the whole world. Except you, Corgan. Too bad for me. I believe in you."

Somehow—and Corgan couldn't tell how it was done—on War Day Minus Two the soldiers seemed more real, like living, breathing, bleeding human beings. To his relief, he began to maneuver them with much less damage. No matter what horrible carnage got hurled at them, or how many devastating weapons exploded in his ears, he moved his troops steadily toward the designated target area with only half as many losses from his own mishandling.

"Splendid, splendid, splendid! You're doing better!" Mendor crooned at the end of the day.

"Now eat everything on your plate and get ready for a good night's sleep."

But Corgan couldn't sleep. The terrible war scenes he'd suppressed all day came flooding at him in the night to haunt him. Children with limbs torn off, lying facedown in bloody mud. Soldiers' bodies, male and female, stacked naked and decaying like fallen leaves.

When he did sleep, bits of lectures he'd heard from Mendor long ago flared into his dreams, in Mendor's stern Father Professor voice. "War is obsolete. We must stop aggressors from taking lives, but we must engage the enemy without killing them."

"So much blood," Corgan wept in his sleep.

"In the old vicious wars, there were no non-combatants: women, children, the innocent, the helpless—all died."

"No. No dying," Corgan tried to cry out, but sleep smothered his cries.

"What was the point of bloody, bloody wars when they were so destructive that nobody won?" Mendor's voice rang through the nightmares. "Even the winners lost."

"No blood!" Corgan moaned, and woke himself from his restless sleep.

"There, there," Mendor the Mother quieted him. "You cried 'no blood.' Of course there will be no blood, Corgan—only in the virtual images. You know that's just pretend."

"But they used to fight like that, didn't they, Mendor? All the killing . . . people really killed each other in the old days, didn't they?"

"Yes. For thousands of years."

"Why did they?"

"Human nature, Corgan. People's instincts can be selfish and ruthless."

"But why do we have to show slaughter in the Virtual War games? Can't we just play a bloodless Virtual War?"

Mendor answered, "There are reasons. You're all sweaty. Let me wipe your face with a cool cloth. Sleep, now. Sleep. It's the middle of the night."

"Two A.M.," Corgan said, "and seven minutes forty-six and nineteen hundredths seconds. But I didn't know the time the other day, Mendor. What if I can't count time again when the War is happening?"

"You'll be fine," she soothed him. "You must trust me, Corgan. This past week, you worked yourself into a state of anxiety over nothing. Didn't you notice how much better you played today? Anyway, tomorrow won't be a hard day. It's the day before the War, and They want you to save your strength. It will be easier tomorrow. Rest now, Corgan. Dream of the Isles of Hiva."

Twelve

"It's time," Mendor whispered, gently shaking Corgan. "This is the day."

He groaned, and fought against waking.

"It's seven in the morning, Corgan."

"I know what time it is, Mendor. I'm the world's most accurate human clock, remember?"

Without touching him, Mendor the Mother Figure wrapped him in a cocoon of love. "Corgan, dear boy, this is the day that may change your life."

"The Isles of Hiva," Corgan murmured. "What will you do if I go there, Mendor?"

Hesitant, she answered, "You won't need me anymore then, so I'll cease to exist."

"I can't imagine you not existing."

Her face hovered over him. She was pale pink, with cheeks so moist and fresh he wanted to touch them, with eyes that radiated love. She said, "If you don't get up now, Corgan, you'll be late for the War, and if you lose the War—no Isles of Hiva. Then the matter of my existence will become irrelevant."

"Right." Wearily, he rolled out of bed and went to sanitize himself in his Clean Room.

Breakfast was tasteless brain-potency-mineral cereal plus some chemical-laden juice that made him gag. "This drink is awful!" he exclaimed.

"It will help your muscles avoid a buildup of lactic acid," Mendor told him. "Save some of it so you can swallow these pills. They're to enhance your synaptic nerve pathways."

"I don't even know what that means," he said, but he took the pills. "I'm ready now," he said.

When he faced Sharla and Brig in the Virtual War Room, their images looked to be so nearby that they could have been within touching distance. But he was inside the confinement of his Box, and they were in their own Boxes, and the Virtual War Room didn't exist except in electronic impulses carried by metal ions embedded in aerogel. No matter how broad the battlefield appeared, no matter how real the soldiers and shells and bombardment and dirt and blood seemed—they were only combinations of light and sound created by clever virtualizers: artists, historians, programmers, and engineers from all three confederations. Those electronic geniuses could pack an entire vast War inside the walls of Corgan's small Box. And inside Sharla's, and Brig's. And the three team members would almost forget they were in separate cubicles; would almost believe they were together. Fighting the War.

"I sense that everyone is prepared," Mendor the Father Figure said. "The Western Hemisphere Federation is counting on the three of you. I know you will fulfill your destiny. Come forward now to stand before the Supreme Council."

Corgan stood up, and watched his virtual image join Sharla's and Brig's in front of the Council table. Subtly at first, then more quickly, the Council members morphed from faceless, identical images into true-to-life representations of Themselves, the way They'd looked when Corgan saw Them, that time, through the transparent wall.

"Since you prefer the look of reality, Corgan . . ." the tall, stooped one said, but he didn't finish the sentence. He just gestured to indicate the others.

Six distinctive, individual right hands raised in a blessing. "Our trust is in you," stated the dissimilar mouths in six unalike though ordinary human faces. "Please recite the pledge."

"I promise," Corgan began, "to wage the War with courage, dedication, and honor." He twisted to get a look at Sharla's lips. Was she saying the real pledge, or was she faking it?

"Take your places now. The countdown begins."

Corgan sat flexing his hands, wondering what exactly had been in the pills Mendor gave him at breakfast. He could feel every nerve ending, each tiny neuron in his arms and fingertips. His hands generated power as he contracted them into fists. Yet each centimeter of his skin had become so sensitive he could feel dust motes that he couldn't even see.

"Eighteen, seventeen, sixteen . . ." Even as the seconds were audibly counted off, Corgan's mind divided them into fragments of hundredths. His internal clock seemed to be working perfectly.

"Begin." The word was spoken so quietly that Corgan might have missed it if his sense of time hadn't been flawless. He waited for the explosion that always signaled the beginning of the practice sessions, but the battlefield stayed so silent he thought the sound effects must have malfunctioned.

Fog rolled in, making it impossible for him to see anything at first. He strained his eyes until he was able to pick out his one hundred soldiers, huddled together in small groups behind camouflage netting.

Then, "On your left!" Brig screamed.

Corgan threw his whole body across the scene and managed to sweep all his troops to safety before the bomb exploded. The blast was so ferocious it shook him physically. It left his ears ringing with such terrible echoes he couldn't hear Brig, who was shouting something and waving his arms, his eyes wide with fear.

Corgan looked up. A heat-seeking missile shrieked toward his troops at such tremendous speed he couldn't hope to save them. Then, too high to cause real damage, it exploded. Sharla! Decoding the trajectory, she'd managed to defuse the warhead. Just in time.

So much heavy artillery flew at Corgan's troops that all he could do was move them out of the way, time after time. Not only was he unable to advance, but his troops kept getting shoved backward, kept losing ground.

"Land mines!" Brig yelled. "Retreat."

"No. I won't." If they did nothing but retreat, there'd be too much ground to make up later. Cupping his hands to intensify the electromagnetic force, he moved his soldiers forward a few at a time, weaving them cautiously across the dangerous minefield for seven minutes forty-two seconds until two mines detonated and three of his troops got blown to bits.

"Do what I say!" Brig screeched. "I'm the Strategist—do you want to lose?"

"Can't help it if there are casualties," Corgan panted, struggling to keep down his breakfast. His stomach heaved at the sight of his soldiers—two men and a young woman with long golden hair— lying entangled in a bloody mess, with the life ripped out of them and seeping into the ground.

"Back! Back!" Brig had to yell to be heard over the rattle of attack rifles. "Now! Around the side, behind that barn!"

"What's the score?" Corgan wanted to know.

"You've lost three. Pacific's lost eight. Eurasia's lost five."

They were ahead! Exultation filled Corgan—he was playing well! At that exact second an armored tank rumbled through the barn, crushing four of his troops. Even as he watched in horror, the tank burst into flame and disintegrated. Sharla again!

Corgan maneuvered his troops into a stand of trees where the fog lay thickest. Again the battlefield fell silent except for muffled explosions in the distance, where Pacific and Eurasia troops were defending themselves. He used the pause to take stock. He'd lost seven soldiers, seven percent of his total force, and he hadn't gained a single meter of ground. He decided to pull his troops into squads of eight: better to realign them, and advance some of the squads toward the target area. Just as he thought of it, Brig said the same thing over the audio connector.

As the hours wore on Corgan wished he could be Brig, who looked down through smoke and flames and fog on the whole picture: at the patterns made when the troops regrouped—his own troops and the ones from the other two confederations. They came together, moved out, died, formed new units, retreated, skirted around buildings and avoided—sometimes—the minefields. Or didn't avoid the minefields and got blown apart.

Corgan's viewpoint was right in the thick of it, at ground level. His hands moved soldiers and when he didn't do it right he watched them die screaming, falling, rising above the earth as their bodies separated into bleeding limbs, torn heads, and eviscerated torsoes.

Brig had stopped shrieking out orders; his commands were now terse and low. At five hours fourteen minutes thirty-seven seconds they had fifty-two troops left, and they were halfway to the target area. Corgan regrouped his squads again—eight soldiers to a squad with four left over for reconnaissance.

It was then he notice his blistered hands. Five hours of compressing electromagnetic energy, nonstop, to move his virtual troops, no matter how gently, had burned the skin on his fingers. He put them into his mouth to suck the blisters, and at that second a bomb killed four more of his troops, four that he could have moved to safety if his hand had been where it was supposed to be instead of in his mouth.

"Damn!" he screamed, and swept his remaining troops inside a barricade, bursting a blister on one of his fingers. There was no stopping to have it cauterized; as Mendor had made abundantly clear, there would be no stopping for anything until exactly five P.M. when the War would end. No food, no water, no wiping away of sweat, and no damage control for raw-skinned team members.

And no Mendor, Corgan realized thankfully. No Mendor to chastise him for whatever stupid mistakes he was making during the course of the War. The team was on its own.

"What score, Brig!" he demanded.

"We have forty-eight troops. Pacific fifty-seven. Eurasia fifty-one."

Corgan groaned aloud. They were down!

"But we're nineteen meters closer to the target area than the other two armies," Brig announced.

So it wasn't totally bad news. Then sweat fell into Corgan's eyes and while he tried to blink away the stinging, a helicopter dropped a fire bomb behind the barricade where three of his squads were waiting.

Forgetting his blistered fingers, forgetting his sweat-stung eyes, Corgan lunged forward to move out what remained of his troops and assess his losses. Two more dead, but that wasn't so bad considering the suddenness of the fire bombing. He advanced them once again to behind the camouflage nets.

Each time a bomb burst, the heat was so searing it made his skin ache. Flares from the explosions blinded him so that he could hardly tell the true colors of anything: All he saw were reverse-color afterimages. The continuous roar deafened him so much he had to try to read Brig's lips, because half the time he couldn't hear the audio connector over the ringing in his ears. Hour after grueling hour the battle raged. Once Corgan used a brief moment's lull to wonder how frail little Brig was managing to hold up. Brig's voice was now a gravelly rasp.

"Sharla says," Brig reported hoarsely at half past three, "we're doing okay."

Corgan wasn't too sure. His fingers had grown numb, and his hands functioned only about half as well as they had when the War started. But by now he had only half as many troops to maneuver.

"Position to target?" he yelled to Brig.

"A hundred and two meters."

So far to go! Corgan wanted nothing more than to lay his head on his arms and blot out the whole bloody battle, but he wiped his eyes with the sleeve of his now-black LiteSuit, and struggled on.

"Brig, report our position to me every five minutes," he ordered. He counted the number of troops remaining to him. Only thirty-seven.

"Wow!" Brig cried hoarsely. "Sharla just threw a code that disabled a huge missile before it even got close to us."

Corgan had no time to worry about Sharla, because he had to maneuver his troops into a ditch. He did it just before another missile streamed over their heads and exploded harmlessly in midair.

"Wow!" Brig cried again. "That was Sharla's doing, too. Wait a minute—she's telling me something. She says—she's broken all the artillery codes. She'll call it out each time they lob some-thing at us so we can cover our troops."

"I've got a better idea. I'll move them between bursts." Again he regrouped his soldiers, this time into parties of three each.

"Now!" Brig called.

Corgan kept his troops down until the artillery passed, then moved a group quickly up the hill.

"Now!" He moved another group.

Each time Brig called out that a shell was com-ing, Corgan moved his soldiers to cover. Then, in the seconds between shellings, he moved them out, one small party after another.

"How much time left?" Brig asked.

"Fourteen minutes seven and . . . bomb!"

Surprised, Corgan realized he'd already moved all his soldiers from the ditch, and he hadn't lost any for the past twelve minutes. "Score, Brig!" he demanded.

"Us thirty-two; Eurasia thirty-seven; Pacific eighteen."

"Distance to target?"

"We're strung out between twelve and twenty-nine meters to target. Consolidate them, Corgan. Uh-oh, Sharla says they figured out she hacked their artillery codes. They've changed crypto keys now. Look out!"

The next bomb found its mark. Corgan lost five soldiers. In another minute one more soldier stepped on a land mine. He was down to twenty-six.

"Sharla's coding to lay down a smoke screen," Brig reported. "Move! Move! Move!"

Under cover of smoke Corgan pulled his twenty-six remaining soldiers into four tight groups, inching them closer to the target area at the top of the hill. He could feel the seconds ticking away; his body vibrated with each fraction of time. Another bomb exploded—two more troops dead. A heat-seeking missile blew up out of range; Sharla had evidently altered its trajectory.

One more minute.

"You're close to target," Brig rasped. "The periphery will be heavily mined. Send the troops in one at a time until you find a safe passage. As soon as one of them gets inside safely, let the others follow the exact same path."

"Okay." He moved one soldier forward. A mine blew her into shreds.

"Use that path!" Brig screamed. "Move your troops one at a time over her body. The mine is already detonated, so that path is safe."

It worked. As the seconds counted down, Corgan propelled his troops one at a time onto the hilltop. At exactly five P.M. he screamed, "Time!"

It was over. Twenty-three Western Hemisphere Federation soldiers were inside the designated area. Twenty-three Eurasian soldiers were also in the area, along with thirteen Pacific troops.

Mendor appeared, to announce, "It's a tie," just as Corgan screamed, "Default!"

The silence was sudden and astonishing, even though Corgan's ears still rang from the explosions.

"No tie!" he cried. "No tie." He could barely speak the words. His lips were cracked dry, his throat swollen almost shut, his tongue raw from grinding his teeth. "Eurasia ran seven hundredths of a second overtime getting their twenty-third soldier across the line. They lose! We win!"

Again silence, but only for eight seconds. Then the War Room erupted in brilliant colors; Corgan could feel the exhilaration. Feel the cheers of triumph. He dragged himself to his feet, grabbed his head with his blistered hands to clear his thoughts, and forced himself back to reality. He was still inside his Box. Everything that had happened had taken place in a world of virtual images while he sat imprisoned in his Box. "Sharla!" he cried.

"Corgan, get back here!" Mendor the jubilant Mother/Father cried. "You're the hero. This is your moment."

He lurched to the wall. "Open the door, Mendor," he rasped, "or I'll shred it into splinters. *I want out!*"

There was no resistance. He fell into the passageway, reeling, staggering from one side to the other of the stainless-steel tunnel until he saw her. She had Brig by the hand. Both of them looked terrible—drained, pale, sweat-stained, tear-stained. With tormented cries the three warriors fell into one another's arms and sobbed.

No one came after them. No one bothered them as they hugged each other and wept, both from the horror of what they'd been through and the joy that they'd won the War.

Sharla rubbed tears from Corgan's face and kissed him on the mouth. "Me too," Brig whimpered. "Me too, Sharla."

She picked him up and kissed his gaunt cheek. The weary Mutant smiled and patted her. Through cracked and swollen lips, he said, "Watch me now! See if I turn into a prince."

Thirteen

The walls of the stainless-steel tunnel pulsed with color as the three of them walked side by side. Color and light.

They'd been given three days to recover from the devastating effects of the War, but Corgan knew he'd never really recover. Every night he woke shaking from terrible dreams—of blood and viscera and shrieks of fear and torn men and women with wide, shocked eyes. His hands still trembled when he ate his excellent meals; they were giving him real eggs now, and as much steak as he could hold. For the first time he'd tasted actual bananas, and if he'd had the stomach for anything, he probably would have liked them. But even the real food soured his mouth.

Nothing much mattered, not even this day, when they were to be honored at some kind or other of award presentation. He hoped the Supreme Council would announce when he and Sharla and Brig could leave for the Isles of Hiva.

They'd been perfectly groomed for the occasion. Their hair had been trimmed, and not just for reasons of sanitation, but to make them look good. All three of them wore matching LiteSuits in shimmering rainbow hues. If Corgan hadn't still been emotionally wasted, he might have felt somewhat happy.

"Could you slow down a little?" Brig asked hoarsely. Brig's skin had a gray pallor, his eyelids were swollen, and his big head shook with a slight tremor. Right after he said that, he stumbled and would have fallen if Corgan hadn't caught him.

"Look, I'm going to carry you till we get to the door, and then you can walk through it when we make our so-called triumphant entrance," Corgan told him.

"Hail! The conquering heroes staggereth in," Brig said. "I just hope it doesn't last too long. I'd like to sleep for about a month."

The wall parted into two doors that rolled back soundlessly. "Enter, please," they heard, and when they moved inside, they saw that they were walking on a red carpet. It extended all the way to the far wall of the room, where the Council members sat on an elevated dais, waiting.

The Council Room was much bigger than it had looked from the outside that night Sharla made the wall transparent. There were no walls or flat ceiling, just a dome covered with a seamless virtual image of wildly cheering people, tens of thousands of them.

"Are they real?" Corgan asked.

Mendor appeared, both male and female. In the tight, confined space of Corgan's Box, Mendor had always loomed large, wrapping around Corgan until he sometimes felt smothered. Here, in this much bigger room, Mendor seemed less real, just one more image among thousands projected on the wall.

"Your fans," he/she said, gesturing around the dome. "Yes, they're real people. Their images are being transmitted here from all the domed cities in the Western Hemisphere Federation. You're their champions."

The Supreme Council members were also real, and not at all electronic: They were bone-and-flesh, living, breathing bodies, warts and whiskers and thinning hair and bad posture and all. Corgan suspected, though, that to the masses of people cheering out there under their domes in their own enclosed cities, wherever they were, the Council members showed only Their usual face-less masks.

"Come forward," They said. One of the Councilwomen stepped out to meet them. In a surprisingly pleasant voice, she said, "Corgan, Sharla, and Brig. You won the War, which means the Western Hemisphere Federation will now take possession of the Isles of Hiva."

At the mention of the Isles, Corgan's fingers twitched.

"But there's more to it than that," the woman continued. "You no doubt wondered why the War was fought so realistically. After all, we could have achieved the same results with a mathematical contest, or a simple athletic event, since the battlefield troops were only virtual images, after all."

Corgan nodded. Sharla didn't.

"The three of you were unaware of it, but every human being in the entire world watched the War being enacted. In all three confederations, every citizen was allowed a work-free day to follow, visually, the progress of the War."

That was a surprise to Corgan.

"It was a reminder," the Council member said, "of what happened when wars used to be fought the old way. It was meant to show why humans can no longer solve disputes by killing one another." Her voice increased in volume, amplified by whatever electronic equipment was broadcasting it. "You three sacrificed yourselves . . ." She paused dramatically. ". . . So that thousands of others will be spared. With the world so sparsely populated now, peace is the only way to achieve survival."

The nearly bald man stood up and began to speak. "Not only are the citizens of the Western Hemisphere grateful to you, but everyone, everywhere in the three confederations is grateful. You young people . . ." He swept his arms in a wide gesture that included the three of them. ". . . May have lost your innocence, but humanity has once again been convinced of the futility of war."

Do I believe that? Corgan wondered. Or are they just empty words to impress those crowds on the wall.

Now the man with the bad slouch took over. "You, Corgan, the team leader, have won your reward," he said. "You will live on the Isles of Hiva for as long as you want."

"Me?" Corgan asked. "All of us! You mean all of us."

Sharla took his hand. "Let Them finish!"

"But he said—"

"We'll talk later!"

"Talk? About what!"

"Please, Corgan," she whispered. "Shut up till it's over."

Corgan didn't care about the gold medal. He didn't pay attention to the speeches, or to the gift of a sixty-year-old pair of blue jeans that one of the Council members told him was what people wore on the Isles of Hiva before they became uninhabitable. When the Council member held them up, the *ooohs* and *aaahs* from the electronic spectators nearly stopped the ceremony. He didn't know why everyone made such a fuss—as if the jeans were some premium bonus or something. To him, they looked pretty faded.

Sharla got a dress of a fabric They called cotton. She seemed pleased, but it probably wouldn't last a tenth as long as a LiteSuit, Corgan thought.

Brig, tired little Brig, got candy. They told him it was real candy made from real sugar—worth as much as the gold medal They'd hung around his neck. Since Brig was so short, the medal hung down a lot lower on him than Corgan's or Sharla's did on them.

Brig held the candy—a sticky red-and-white-striped rod thirty centimeters high—then licked his fingers. *"Mmmmm,"* he said, his eyes brightening. He broke off a piece of it for Sharla, but Corgan refused any.

Let's get this over with, Corgan said inside his mind. Inside his chest, a heavy weight kept growing as each minute passed. He needed to find out what that Councilman had meant when he mentioned Hiva.

One at a time, the Supreme Council came up to shake the team's hands; Brig was standing on a chair between Sharla and Corgan. The Council members kept saying congratulatory things, and Brig and Sharla answered nicely with all the right phrases, but Corgan just mumbled, "Thank you," over and over.

After the Council retreated to hide once again behind their electronic disguises, ordinary people from the city were allowed into the room. They streamed past Sharla and Brig and Corgan, gushing about how the three of them were heroes and were a real inspiration to young children and grown-ups, too. Why was the Council letting those people into the chambers? Didn't anyone worry about contamination anymore? It seemed to go on and on, people Corgan had never seen before filing past to look at him like he was some kind of curiosity. Some even reached out to touch him—his LiteSuit, his arm—all the while they were mouthing words of praise Corgan didn't listen to. Why wouldn't they just go away?

Then he recognized Jobe.

"Hey, you guys," Jobe cried. "You did really great!"

"Thanks, Jobe," Sharla answered.

"I just got a copy of the game stats," Jobe said, waving a sheaf of papers. "You know, you didn't make a single error. Not one infraction of the rules, not even by accident."

Corgan whipped around to glance at Sharla. That was the first confirmation he'd heard that she hadn't cheated. She raised her eyebrows and smiled wryly, as if to tell him: So it's official. To Jobe she said, "What can we say? We're just good, that's all."

"Well, hey, I want to thank you all," Jobe went on. "I picked up a bundle on that game. My buddies here—see these guys behind me? I told them I'd bring them here to meet you." Two burly men shuffled and grinned, peering around Jobe to get a good look at the team.

Jobe's words pierced through Corgan's indifference, although he wasn't sure what they meant.

"Anyway," Jobe went on, "before you guys played the War, these here guys said, 'No team can play eight whole hours without any errors,' and I told them, 'Hey, I know Sharla and Corgan and Brig. I've met them personally. I know they can do it.' So I told my buddies, 'If you don't think so, put your money where your mouth is.' And they did, and I won big!"

"Wait a minute." Now Corgan was staring intently at him. "You mean you bet on the War?"

"Sure. Everybody did—well, maybe not everybody—"

"You bet on the War!" Never in his life had Corgan felt such a surge of rage. It swept up from his chest to throb in his ears. He could taste it in his mouth. *"You bet on the War?"*

"Yeah, well—it was a game, wasn't it?"

Corgan stormed, "All those people *died* so you could *bet*?"

"People! They were nothing but—"

Corgan's fists slashed out before Jobe could say any more.

"Corgan!" Sharla screamed.

He punched Jobe's face till blood spurted from the man's lips, then pounded his soft gut until Jobe's buddies grabbed Corgan and pinned his arms behind him.

Brig shouted, "Take your friends and get out of

here, Jobe. And lock the doors behind you."

"What's the disturbance?" Mendor the Father Figure demanded, his image looming large on the wall behind them. Several members of the Council crowded forward, asking, "What is it? Is something wrong?"

"It's nothing. Would you kindly have the room cleared now?" Brig asked Them. "We'd appreciate it."

As soon as Corgan stopped struggling, the two men let him loose—releasing his arms slowly, but standing poised to grab him if he started swinging again. Corgan stayed passive, head lowered, fists clenched.

Backing up awkwardly, the men led away the bleeding Jobe, who held a cloth against his lips. One of his friends muttered, "You know these athletes. They get real stressed out after a big game. It's normal."

"But he *won*!" Jobe protested. "So why'd he go all freaky? It was only a game—not like a real war or anything. . . ."

Hesitantly, the Councilwoman with the pleasant voice said, "Are you all right now, Corgan? Would you like to stay here with your teammates for a while? You three may stay as long as you wish."

"Alone?" Sharla asked.

"Certainly. If you wish."

Morphed once again between male and female, Mendor asked, "Do you want me to leave, too, Corgan?"

"Yes I do."

Reluctantly, Mendor disappeared, and then they *were* alone. Corgan rubbed his shoulder, which throbbed with pain from being twisted by Jobe's buddies.

"Does it hurt?" Sharla asked. "Jobe and his friends—they just don't understand, Corgan. How the War was the most important part of our whole lives for so long—"

"Forget that!" he barked. "There's something a lot more important going on. I want to know what."

"You mean about the betting?" Brig asked.

"Dammit, you know what I mean! About the Isles of Hiva."

Sharla and Brig glanced at each other, questioning which of them would answer first. "I'm sorry it turned out like this," Sharla said. "We should have talked yesterday, or the day before, but Brig was exhausted—"

"So talk now!"

Brig began. "It was strategy. Your game was off. The Council called Sharla and me to a meeting. They asked if we could suggest some reward for you that might make you play better."

Taking over, Sharla said, "They told us if we could figure out an incentive that would improve your game, then we could name any reward we wanted for ourselves, too."

Anguished, Corgan cried, "Hiva was supposed to be for all three of us!"

"There are bigger things, Corgan," Brig said. "When They asked me what my greatest wish would be, I took a chance and said, 'If You'll let the Mutants live, I know I could work with them. I can make their lives better.'"

"That's it? That's what you asked for?"

Brig was obviously weary. "Look at me, Corgan. Do I look like I could run along a beach or go plunging into the ocean at Hiva? I don't want to spend what's left of my life lying under a tree on the sand watching *you*. Anyway, to sum it all up, They said yes. They'll let the Mutants live."

Corgan didn't know how to answer. It was almost overwhelming, that weak little Brig had been able to pull off something that big.

"It'll be the toughest strategy I'll ever have to devise, trying to make the Mutants useful. But at least I know I can improve their lives. And they'll *have* lives now. They won't be put to sleep like unwanted kittens." Brig lowered himself and stretched out on two folding chairs, saying, "Sorry, boys and girls, I really need a nap. Wake me when this is all over."

Taking the cotton dress They'd given her, Sharla spread it over Brig to keep him warm. Then, with her finger to her lips, she gestured for Corgan to follow her to the far end of the room.

"I'm seriously worried about Brig," she told Corgan. "He was never strong to begin with, and the War really wasted him." She sat on the floor, tucking her feet beneath her, and gestured for Corgan to sit beside her. But he wouldn't.

Crouched above her, wretched and disillusioned, Corgan cried, "I'm the one who feels wasted! I can't believe how you tricked me. I trusted you."

"Maybe you shouldn't have trusted me. I told you I didn't care anything about honor."

With his back against the wall, he stared down at her. "I never know what to believe about you. At least when I trusted you not to cheat, you didn't. The stats proved that."

After a moment she answered, "Everyone was worried about your slump, Corgan. They were trying to motivate you."

"They must have thought I was pretty stupid to be jerked around like that."

"Not stupid. Just innocent." She reached up, took his hand, and pulled him, resisting, down beside her. "Think about it, Corgan—would you have tried so hard to win Hiva if you'd known I wouldn't live there? That's why They didn't tell you."

He shook his head. "So it was NNTK all over again."

"No. 'No Need To Know' is a lot different from 'Don't let him find out.' It was all part of the conspiracy of silence—don't ask, don't tell, just win the War."

Straightening his back, he said, "Yeah, well, you can just think about *this*! All your lies and scheming were for nothing. I came out of the slump, and I did it by myself."

Again she was silent. Then, "You're right. How did you do it?"

He gave a bitter, ironic laugh. "I was *motivated* because I didn't want you to have to cheat. But even more important . . ."

"What?"

"It was . . ." His voice broke. "What you said. When you told me you believe in me."

"Oh, Corgan!" She leaned forward to lay her head against his shoulder, and he didn't pull away.

Once again her presence, the scent of her, the feel of her body against his, of her hair against his skin, made his heart pound in spite of his damaged illusions. "It was easier when I lived inside a Box," he said. "Being told what to do, what to think. Real life is too messy. People are too complicated. The real world isn't worth all the trouble."

"Give it a chance," she said.

He leaned his head back against the wall and watched the room's muted colors pulse in ever-changing, fluid shapes. Beautiful reflections, and that's all they were. Not reality. "One thing's sure," he told her. "I could never stand to go back inside a Box. Not anymore. Now I'm not sure where I belong."

"On Hiva," she answered.

That made the ache come back again. "So what did you request for your reward?" he asked.

She stirred against his arm and sat up to face him. "An automated DNA sequencing machine. There's a really powerful one in a place called Nebraska, just sitting there useless because it's full of contamination."

"That means They can't get it for you, right?" In the room's indirect, pulsing luminescence, her golden hair shimmered with highlights, the way it had the first day he ever saw her.

"They promised They would. They'll send out a squad of robots to get the sequencer, decontaminate it, and find some kind of passable roads to transport it here."

"Sounds pretty major," he said.

"It'll take at least six months, They told me. But it's worth it, Corgan—it's an incredible machine. It can detect mutations at the two-cell level, before the cells even start to divide."

He asked, "Does that mean there won't be any more Mutants?"

"There'll always be some born naturally, outside the lab. Brig will have plenty of work to do. Anyway, even using the sequencer to analyze DNA, I'll need years to discover anything valuable." She smiled. "I can't wait to start. Decoding human DNA is the ultimate goal. At least for me it is." She lowered her eyes and said, "I decided I'd do anything to get it. Even lie to you, Corgan. I'm sorry."

As she moved closer to him, he winced from

the pain in his twisted shoulder. "Does it still hurt that much?" Sharla asked him. "Let me rub it for you."

He leaned forward to let her get behind him and massage his shoulder. Unable to see her face, Corgan asked, "So! What are you planning to do for the six months it takes to get your machine here?"

Her strong fingers kneaded his muscles, but they stopped. Seven and nineteen hundredths seconds passed before she answered, "Well, I thought I'd . . . go with you to the Isles of Hiva. If you want me to. Do you?"

Forgetting his pain, Corgan squeezed his eyes shut. He said, "Yes."

Fourteen

Corgan was bloody up to his elbows. His strong hands groped inside the warm body, grasping, tugging, as the cow bellowed her outrage and pain.

"I have to twist it," he told Sharla. "I don't want to hurt it—wait! Wait. I feel the head. It's coming out now. Stand back." In a rush of fluid the calf fell into his arms.

Corgan laughed out loud as he stood the calf on its wobbly legs and pulled off what was left of the placenta. "She's alive. She's beautiful!" Pointing to his own blood-soaked blue jeans and manure-caked boots, he said, "And I'm filthy. But who cares?"

After he rubbed the calf with a rough towel, its brown and white hair stood up in little whorls.

Sharla asked, "Do you need to let the lab team know right away that the calf has been born?"

"No hurry," he told her. "They can do the blood test later. I'm going to leave her with her mother for a while."

"Look at those big brown eyes," Sharla murmured. "Even if she isn't transgenic, even if she turns out to be just a plain ordinary cow, she's darling."

But it will be a lot better if she *is* transgenic, Corgan thought. With the arrival of each new calf, the genetics team kept hoping. So far they'd created just two calves that carried a special human gene resistant to the Ebola virus. Maybe this new baby would be the third.

A blood sample and a simple genetic test would confirm—or dash—the hopes of the team. If the calf was transgenic, it meant the team had succeeded in implanting the human gene into the fertilized ovum, and the cow would grow up to produce milk containing a human protein. Extracted from the milk, the protein from one cow could stop an Ebola outbreak in a whole domed city. Protein from two dozen transgenic cows would be able to cure an epidemic worldwide. And Ebola was just a starter. The genetics researchers— the people who shared a laboratory on the northern end of the island—had already recombined genes to counteract every major plague virus. If their work eventually succeeded, Earth could become habitable again. But so far, only two out of sixty-one newborn calves had turned out to be transgenic.

"As long as you don't have to report the calf's birth right away," Sharla said, "let's go down to the beach. You really ought to wash all that . . . stuff . . . off you."

"What, you don't like mud, and blood, and—" Corgan grinned at her, bent his knee, and pointed to the heel of his boot. "This nice 'stuff' on my boots? Maybe you don't know the right word for it. Let me improve your vocabulary, Sharla. This 'stuff,' this cow by-product, is called—"

Her laughter rang out, that wonderful, rich, delicious laugh that Corgan loved. "Never mind. I know what it's called. Just leave the boots here."

Both of them ran barefoot from the top of the hill, where the barn stood, all the way to the beach. Corgan could easily have outraced Sharla because he was the faster runner, but he liked to stay behind her where he could watch her free, graceful movements.

Six months' worth of bleaching from the tropical sun, six months of salt spray from the ocean, six months' wear and tear from sand, and Sharla's cotton dress had become tattered. She insisted on wearing it that day even though she'd grown taller and the dress had shrunk and torn at the hem.

Corgan's blue jeans had suffered almost as much. They were torn, faded, frayed, and stained from the work he'd been doing. Since he hadn't been given a shirt to go with the jeans, he went bare-chested most of the time. His skin had turned far darker from the sun than Sharla's, because Corgan was brunette, something he'd never even thought about when he lived inside the Box where there was no real sun.

They raced into the surf and splashed each other until Corgan had completely cleaned himself of the cow's birth matter and the spatters of manure on the legs of his jeans. Then they swam together, floating where the surf carried them.

He pulled her to her feet so he could always remember her the way she was now, as they stood there in the shallow water, the waves lapping their ankles. Sharla looked golden. Sun had streaked her hair countless different shades of gold, some of them exactly matching her skin.

Waves crashed around them, pushing them forward and then pulling them back when the water returned to its bed in the sea. This was the real roar of the real ocean they were hearing, so much more powerful than artificial noises filtered through electronic signals and aerogel.

Sharla's dress clung to her. When she shivered, Corgan took her hand and led her out of the surf.

"Look," she said, pointing at the sand.

They knelt to examine a jellyfish washed up by the waves. It lay stranded on the sand, brown, shiny, and gelatinous, like an overturned bowl with a dark fringe around the edges.

"You can see inside it," Corgan exclaimed, pointing to narrow coils of viscera, and to the thin, delicate strands of tissue that showed beneath the transparent surface membrane.

"Primitive and perfect," Sharla announced. "We've evolved, and they've stayed the same."

"Let's figure out a way to move it so we can toss it back into the ocean. It'll die here in the sun."

"No, Corgan," she said, pulling on his arm. "Don't interfere with nature. The waves washed it up, so—"

His bark of laughter was incredulous. "You don't want me to interfere with nature? And *you're* going back to slice up DNA and engineer humans! While *I* stay here, birthing genetically altered calves that might save what's left of humanity."

Sinking down, she patted the sand for him to sit beside her. "We only have a little while before I have to leave. Let's not waste it talking shop. No ideas deeper than . . . than the foam on the surf."

Corgan sprawled on the beach and looked out at the waves. He loved the way they rolled up and melted the sand from beneath his bare feet. Taking Sharla's hand, he pressed it into the damp surface. The imprint of her palm and fingers stayed just out of reach of the foam-flecked water. Then he imprinted his own hand, with the indentations of his fingers meshing into hers.

"I'll miss you," she said.

"Your things are already packed, and the Harrier Jet won't take off for about an hour," he told her. "You don't have to leave just yet." He remembered his own flight in the Harrier Jet when the panels of the domed city had opened to allow the aircraft to rise, straight up, out of the only place he'd ever known till that time. At six thousand meters' altitude the aircraft had turned southwest. It was then that Corgan saw, for the first time, snow-covered mountain peaks, and actual trees, and lakes that reflected sunlight and made his breath catch with their beauty.

Sharla said, "You never even mention minutes anymore, Corgan, let alone fractions of seconds."

"Why should I? I work with cattle now. All that matters to animals is seasons, not seconds." Digging another imprint in the sand with his fingers, he said, "There's something else different about me, too. Look."

He held up his hands. They were rough and splintered, with the fingernails ragged and none too clean. "I remember," he said, "at the celebration, when I hit Jobe—all I could think of was that I didn't have to worry about my hands anymore. I could split my knuckles on his face, and no one would care."

Sharla smiled. "Jobe cared! The poor guy—he never knew what he did wrong."

After a while they stood up to walk back toward the Western Hemisphere Biotechnology Laboratory, keeping close, holding hands. The sun warmed them. He ached because he knew she was leaving him. She'd stayed with him nearly every minute for six months, cheering him when he delivered a calf, helping him learn to be comfortable with the genetic scientists in the laboratory. Sometimes he needed to get away, to go off by himself, but he was getting better at socializing, Sharla told him. Getting used to people.

"They like you," she said. "They love telling you about their work because you listen and you learn so fast."

"It's interesting stuff," he'd answered. "It's like finally understanding how and why I got started in a test tube. Me and the calves—we're mutations with a purpose."

Since both Corgan and Sharla had been born in the laboratory on the same day, they'd celebrated their fifteenth birthdays together, running on the beach. They'd played a real game of Go-ball with real racquets and a real ball, using a line drawn in the sand for their net.

Now, on her last day on the Isles of Hiva, they approached the laboratory. The roof of the narrow, single-story building had been thatched with palm fronds in the same way the natives had thatched their huts so long ago, or so he'd been told.

"Have you heard any news about Brig?" Corgan asked.

"He's in bad shape. He can't walk at all now, but he keeps working on his programs for the Mutants. I'll see him tomorrow."

"Tell him I said . . ." What message could he send to Brig? Nothing seemed adequate.

"I'll give him your love," Sharla promised. "Do you want to wait here? I'll just be a minute inside the building. I need to change into my LiteSuit and pick up my bag for the flight."

"I'll wait," he told her. The Harrier Jet would leave in a few minutes from the concrete launch pad two hundred meters away. Corgan could hear the jet engines warming up. To find out if he could still do it, he tried to count the revolutions-per-second of the engines just by listening to them throb, but his ability to calculate time had fallen off. He was no longer split-second accurate.

When Sharla came out of the building, they walked toward the launch pad. "I almost hate to leave Hiva. It's so beautiful here," she murmured. "Everything is! I understand why Gauguin wanted to paint it all."

"Who's Gauguin?" he asked, raising his voice when they approached the aircraft.

"A French artist who came here two hundred years ago. These islands were called the Marquesas then. He painted the people and the ocean and these very same palm trees, or at least the ancestors of these trees."

"Ancestors," he mused. "Everything has them, one way or another. Trees, humans, cows—"

"That reminds me." Speaking loudly now, she turned toward him. "Listen, Corgan, when you're putting together your statistical data on the trans-genic cattle, be careful."

"Careful? Why?"

In one hand, Sharla carried the small bag that

held her clothes; in the other hand, a pink hibiscus blossom to remind her of Hiva. She backed slowly across the concrete pad, still facing Corgan. When he attempted to follow her, the pilot waved him away and shook his head, meaning Corgan couldn't come any closer.

"Don't always believe statistics," Sharla shouted. "Statistics can be tweaked to prove almost anything. Genetic stats, population stats, War-game stats!"

He frowned, trying to understand the words he had trouble hearing over the engine roar. "Wait a minute! What are you—Sharla?"

The engines revved to a higher pitch. Sharla climbed a small ladder to reach the open hatch of the cockpit, then turned and waved.

At the top of his voice Corgan cried out, "Sharla! The game stats! Did you—"

"NNTK, Corgan."

"Sharla!" Not caring about his own safety, Corgan ran toward the Harrier Jet.

"'Bye, Corgan! Enjoy your Isles of Hiva that you love so much! I'll be back some day." She slid into the seat behind the pilot just before the hatch closed above her.

The aircraft rose vertically, lifting straight up into the perfect sky. Corgan ran after it until there was nothing left to see. Sharla was gone.

Alone, he stood on the empty beach.

Read the First Book in the Virtual War Chronologs
VIRTUAL WAR

Imagine a life of virtual reality—a childhood contained in a controlled environment, with no human contact or experiences outside of the world of computer-generated images.

Corgan has been genetically engineered by the Federation for quick reflexes, high intelligence, and physical superiority. Everything Corgan is, everything he has ever seen or done, was to prepare him for one moment: a bloodless, computer-controlled virtual war.

When Corgan meets his two fellow warriors, he begins to question the Federation. Now Corgan must decide where his loyalties lie, what he's willing to fight for, and exactly what he wants in return. His decisions will affect not only these three virtual warriors, but all the people left on earth.

LaVergne, TN USA
01 October 2009
159539LV00001B/7/P